ELLEN ELIZABETH HUNTER

MURDER AT THE AZALEA FESTIVAL

A "Murder in Wilmington" Mystery

Magnolia Mysteries

Greensboro, North Carolina

This is a work of fiction.

Published by Magnolia Mysteries
P.O. Box 38041
Greensboro, North Carolina 27438

ISBN: 0-9755404-1-6

Book design by Jeff Pate
Cover design by Tim Doby

Second Printing

Also by Ellen Elizabeth Hunter

Murder on the Candlelight Tour (2003)

Murder on the Ghost Walk (2004)

Visit Ellen's website,
www.ellenhunter.com
Or contact her at:
ellenelizabethhunter@earthlink.net

Acknowledgements

I am grateful to many wise and generous people for helping me to make the "Murder in Wilmington" series a success.

To the booksellers and librarians—Becky Carignan, Barnes & Noble, Greensboro; Nicki Leone, Bristol Books, Wilmington; Sarah Goddin, Quail Ridge Books, Raleigh; Sarah Carr and Feebe Fitch of McIntyre's Fine Books in Fearrington Village; Sheila and MJ of The Heller Bookery; Terri Hill, The Book Stop, High Point; Dorothy Hodder, New Hanover County Public Library; Beth Sheffield, Carol Humble, and Ron Headen of the Greensboro Public Library—a big THANK YOU for getting my books out there and into the hands of mystery lovers.

To Cathy Boettcher of the Lower Cape Fear Historical Society, a heartfelt thanks for giving *Murder on the Candlelight Tour* a special place on the real Candlelight Tour. Cathy, you gave me wings.

A special thank you to Beverly Tetterton, Special Collections Librarian, New Hanover County Public Library, for proofreading the first draft of *Murder at the Azalea Festival* and for sharing her insider's knowledge of Wilmington with me. BT, you're awesome!

Thanks also to my mystery author pals, Radine Trees Nehring, Dorothy P. O'Neill, and Nancy Gotter Gates, for your friendship, support, and thoughtful critiques.

For fascinating revelations and a factual account of life on the Cape Fear in the 1800s, I must credit Professor David S. Cecelski's *The Waterman's Song*. Richard Price's *Maroons: Rebel Slaves in the Americas*, and David Walker's *Appeal to the Coloured Citizens of the World* provided insight and inspiration relating to the history of that era.

And to my niece Tiffany Nicole Talliere, thank you for letting me borrow your beautiful name.

This book is dedicated to my granddaughter, Olivia,
and to the men in my life, Gary and James.

1

"Ashley, where have you been?" Jon Campbell asked. "I can't believe you haven't heard that three bodies washed ashore at Fort Fisher! The first was on Sunday, another on Monday, then the third yesterday."

On the Wednesday of Azalea Festival week, Jon and I were driving south on River Road. Jon is an architect. I'm Ashley Wilkes, a historic preservationist. We work together restoring old houses and were on our way to inspect Moon Gate, a crumbling Greek Revival mansion with a mysterious past.

"I've been busy," I said in my defense. "Interviewing clients, evaluating properties. I'm not a news junkie!"

The truth was I'd been in a funk—what Holly Golightly called the "mean reds"—ever since I learned that the love of my life homicide detective Nick Yost had returned to Wilmington; he hadn't even given me a call. Keeping my chin up off the ground was what I'd been doing all week. I'd buried myself in work.

"So, tell me about it," I invited, gazing idly out the window of Jon's Jeep Cherokee at the flowering dogwoods and redbuds. Wild pink azaleas grew right up to the road, as plentiful as orange daylilies in summer.

Fueled with excitement about the drownings, Jon said, "There's been something about it in the *Star-News* every day, and the TV stations have been broadcasting live from the scene. The police say the bodies are male, but they don't know who they are. And if they know the cause of death, they aren't saying. The newscasters refer to them as homicides."

"Well, I've been too busy pouring through archives, researching Moon Gate to bother with watching the news," I replied.

Jon continued, "The sheriff has formed a special task force to investigate the unexplained deaths."

That got my attention. "So that's why Nick is back in town!" I exclaimed.

"Nick's back?" Jon asked.

"Melanie saw him and told me."

Melanie is my older sister, Melanie Wilkes, realtor *extraordinaire*. Mama was besotted with *Gone With the Wind*, naming us girls after Margaret Mitchell's characters. We've often laughed that it was a good thing we didn't have a brother, for surely Mama would have named him Rhett Butler Wilkes!

Right after Christmas, homicide detective Nick Yost had transferred from the Wilmington Police Department to Atlanta PD's cold case task force. We'd promised to stay in touch and visit on weekends.

In January he'd kept his part of the bargain with long "missing you" and "needing you" telephone calls and occasional e-mails. As he got more and more immersed in his cases, the calls and e-mails dwindled to a stop, and he did not respond to the messages I left on his voice mail.

Throughout February, I checked my e-mail a dozen times a day, his picture propped on my desk so I could moon over it as I prayed for a hotmail message. A dozen times a day, I experienced disappointment.

When the hurt became too acute to bear, I stopped looking for e-mails, gave up on prayers, stashed his picture in a desk drawer under a pile of papers. What does it mean when one face is the only one you long to see? When no other face will do? Is it love? Or obsession?

I mustered self-discipline from somewhere and went back to checking my e-mails twice a day in a business-like fashion. On the surface, I was the same, good-old Ashley, but inside I felt like someone was ripping my heart out.

One good thing came of this experience, I lost seven pounds. My normally robust appetite disappeared, and along with it my chunky waistline. Melanie's been nagging me to go shopping for new clothes. She objects to what she calls my "construction-wear chic."

"So Nick took a leave of absence from Atlanta PD to help out here," Jon said thoughtfully. "And he hasn't called you?"

"No," I said softly.

"Well then, it's because he's busy, Ashley. But he will just as soon as he gets a breather. Those cases have got the authorities baffled. If the police don't solve this by Memorial Day, the summer tourist season will take a beating. Who wants to bring the kiddies to the beach if there's any danger a corpse might wash up?"

"I'm sure you're right, Jon," I said with a determination I didn't feel. "He's busy, that's it." But in my heart I wasn't convinced. No one was that busy.

Jon shook his blonde head. "I know how you feel. I just learned that Christine is getting married."

"Married?"

"Yeah, some marine biologist she met in graduate school. They're going up to Maine to save the whales, or whatever."

"How could she know anyone well enough to marry him when she's been dating you since December? I have to tell you, Jon, the two of us—we have a knack for picking fickle lovers."

"Well, obviously," Jon said bitterly, "she was dating him too. Only I, sucker that I am, didn't suspect a thing. I'm swearing off women forever."

I reached over from the passenger seat to pat his arm. "I hope you aren't including me in that vow."

"You? Of course not. We're friends. How long have we been working together now? A year and a half? I trust you. But other women? They're so devious."

"Well, I'm sorry. You're way too good for any woman to treat so shabbily."

How could she dump him? I wondered as I studied his profile. He's a sweetheart, one of the last true Southern gents. And a real hunk with golden blonde hair, a ruddy complexion from working out of doors, laughing brown eyes that shine with sincerity and truthfulness. Jon's as transparent as a bride's negligee, an easy target for an unscrupulous woman. I'd have to keep an eye on him—on both of us from now on. A couple of softies, that's what we are.

I wanted to wrap my arms around him and give him a big hug but that was impossible in our divided seats. "I know what," I said, "let's do the festival together. Want to? There's a shag contest on Saturday?"

That should tempt him. Jon loves to shag.

"Suits me," he replied. "I'm free for most of the festivities."

"Then it's settled; we'll go together. But it'll be mobbed. There were more than 350,000 people here last year, but they bring in the big bucks, $5 million, at last count."

We followed the course of the Cape Fear in silence, each of us reflecting about our lost loves. Under the sunny April sky, the river was broad and majestic, sparkling with ribbons of silver and gold. In the days before radar and other navigational marvels, it had been a dangerous body of water. First called Charles, then Clarendon, eventually it was named Cape Fear after the treacherous cape at its mouth, the Cape of Fear, a sandy shoal that shifted unpredictably, capsizing ships and striking terror in the hearts of sailors.

"They're dredging the shipping channel," Jon said. "Deepening it from 38 to 42 feet."

As we drove alongside the 300 acre State Port, I spotted the giant gantry crane the port authority had installed in the fall. It was huge and white and reminded me of a praying mantis.

Further out in the shipping lane, the dredge rose, red and raw and skeletal, with a scoop-like mechanism that dredged sand from the bottom of the river and deposited it onto a barge. The barge would ferry the sand to an offshore disposal area. Eventually it would be deposited on Bald Head Island's South Beach.

"They had a real knock-down drag-out over who would get the renourishment sand," he continued. "Caswell Beach and Oak Island had been promised the sand, but Bald Head Island wanted it too, claiming the harbor project was eroding Bald Head's South Beach."

"All the beaches are eroding, Jon. Every major hurricane carves out a new channel."

"The Army Corps of Engineers argued just that point, that South Beach is historically a fluctuating shoreline, but when the debate turned to who might sue, they found themselves stuck between a rock and a hard place."

"I've been to South Beach," I said. "It's been sandbagged since the nineties."

"Who knows when the project will be completed," Jon said.

Passing the Beau Rivage golf course on our left, I craned my neck for glimpses of scarlet azaleas.

"Okay, the Talliere place is coming up soon," I cautioned, "only the road's not marked, so it's easy to miss. Slow down after this curve. There, that's it. Turn right there."

Jon steered into a narrow, paved driveway.

"Last week when I was out here," I said, "this was little more than a rutted lane. It had to be paved to accommodate the Azalea Festival garden tour."

"I'm anxious to see the restored gardens," Jon commented. "It's been ages since I've been out here. Sure is remote."

"You'll be impressed. The Tallieres used to have a reputation as recluses. Tiffany has changed all that. She's determined to restore the house to its original state, and that's where we come in. Lordy, that house is going to be one stupendous challenge for us, Jon; the family has really let that place go."

"But that means there will have been few improvements. The architecture will be pure; no fake ceilings to remove," Jon said.

"True. A restorationist's dream house. Tiffany's also determined to restore the Tallieres to society. And bringing Caesar Talliere's terraced gardens back to life and putting them on the tour was the first step. She and her brother are not clannish like their ancestors. They're open and friendly. She's really made a name for herself in television. There's an Emmy in that girl's future."

Tiffany Nicole Talliere, an actress on an evening soap called *Dolphin's Cove*, was twenty years old. The show was a hot new TV series, set in the fictitious town of Dolphin's Cove, a town very similar to Wilmington; most scenes were shot locally. The cast were twenty-somethings playing at being seventeen. The story-line featured a group of high school seniors, four girls and four boys, who frequently fell in and out of love with each other. Adolescents on the brink of adulthood, they faced the challenges of college admission and living away from home for the first time.

"There's the moon gate," I said as we approached a circular gate set in a high, crumbling brick wall.

Ancient oaks and understory grew right up to the road. Through the trees I caught glimpses of the eerie, swampy cypress gardens.

2

After passing a dilapidated carriage house, the Talliere mansion came into view. My restorationist's eye took in the disrepair. "Yes, we've really got our work cut out for us, Jon. This isn't going to be easy."

"You can say that again. I had no idea this place was so run down. I can't even remember the last time I was out here."

"I don't think much has been done since Caesar's day," I remarked. "And that was a hundred and thirty years ago. I don't know how the Talliere descendants managed to hang on here."

"Besides Tiffany and her brother, who's left? Didn't their parents die in an Amtrak crash? Something tragic, like that?"

"Yes, a train wreck. Now there's only the two of them left."

Jon continued, "There's a rumor that during Prohibition, this was the place to buy whiskey. With the isolation out here and a private boat dock, some of the Tallieres survived by smuggling whiskey."

"Well, Tiffany and Auguste are different," I said. "They want this to be a comfortable home again. Now that there's an infusion of capital in the Talliere coffers, they're determined to re-establish the family's good name. And volunteering Caesar's gardens for the Azalea Festival Tour is a clever move."

"Auguste's the brother?" Jon asked as he parked the Cherokee in the newly-paved circular drive in front of the house.

"He is. I haven't met him yet. He was out of the country when Tiffany and I had our meetings, but she says he's committed. Actually, he's her half-brother, my age, twenty-five, and Tiffany calls him Gus. They seem devoted to each other."

I pulled down the sun visor to check my face in the mirror. We'd spent the morning crawling around an old house downtown and I felt grimy and rumpled.

My dark brown hair was curlier than it normally is, thanks to a brief spring shower. I pulled a cobweb off a curl, freshened my lipstick, and blinked at myself in the mirror. My eyes are gray, but in a certain light they look violet.

Stepping down from the Jeep, I adjusted the faded denim shirt I wore unbuttoned over a white tee shirt, and brushed off my khaki shorts. I had on construction boots with heavy socks because there's always the danger of stepping on a rusty nail in an old house.

The Talliere mansion rose before us, white and sprawling. Its architectural style was Greek Revival. Caesar Talliere built it for his bride Lucy in 1870 during the height of his prosperous shipbuilding career.

Eighteen-seventy was a little late for the Greek Revival style, but according to Tiffany, when Caesar arrived in Wilmington for the first time and saw the glorious white mansions, he promised himself that one day he'd have his own.

The original central section featured a classic portico with pediment. Two symmetrical wings on either side were added later as the Talliere progeny increased. Piazzas connected the wings to the main section, lending the mansion a tropical feel, and they probably did catch breezes off the Cape Fear during the worst of our steamy summers.

The mansion was literally falling apart. Glass panes were missing from a few of the windows. The white paint on the wood-frame structure was graying and streaked with mildew, whole patches worn away, exposing bare and rotting wood.

We were high on a bluff overlooking the Cape Fear where mighty live oaks dripped with Spanish moss and cast a dappled shade over the upper gardens. Between the house and the gardens, magnolias had grown tall and strong over the years.

I regarded the terraced gardens that descended to the river. The air smelled of English boxwoods, an astringent scent I love, and indeed there were hundreds of them and they had grown as tall as a man and were over a century in age. They delineated the formal pathways that descended to the lagoon and a wildfowl refuge.

In all directions, one saw a thousand flowering azaleas, at their peak and covered with scarlet, white, fuchsia, and lilac blossoms.

Off to the left and about midway down the bluff, another moon gate had been installed in a brick wall that enclosed a private garden where many species of camellia flourished.

Beyond, a Chinese bridge crossed the lagoon. I caught sight of an alligator floating lazily in the murky water. In the tall grass at the lagoon's edge, a blue heron stood as still as a statue. Somewhere nearby, mourning doves cooed softly.

The front door opened and Tiffany bounced out onto the portico, dwarfed by immense Corinthian columns. "Hi," she called, waving and skipping down the semi-circular steps.

Jon seemed mesmerized and I nudged him forward.

A man appeared behind her, strolling from the house at a leisurely pace, and I assumed he was Auguste. He had on a bright white dress shirt, collar open, sleeves rolled up on his forearms. His hands were stuffed into jeans pockets, not an easy accomplishment since the jeans were tight. My girlish antennae began to quiver. I'm sick of those low-slung, baggy pants men wear these days. If a man's got it, he ought to flaunt it, is my philosophy. Those guys with their baggy britches could be eunuchs for all we girls could see.

Tiffany was the epitome of wholesomeness, with her breezy girl-next-door looks. Her glossy dark brown hair swung around her shoulders; brown eyes were lively and crinkled at the corners when she smiled as she did now. The smile lit up her face. It was that engaging smile that had made her a favorite with the fans of *Dolphin's Cove*. She had on white shorts and a red tee shirt and her legs were deeply tanned, athletic yet shapely.

Reaching my side, she put her hands on my shoulders and kissed me on the cheek. "Ashley, I'm so glad to see you."

Extending a hand to Jon, she said in the friendly voice that was familiar to the millions who were hooked on *Dolphin's Cove*, "And you must be Jon Campbell."

Jon took her hand and for a second seemed tongue-tied. "Yeah, that's me. Glad to meet you, Tiffany."

Was he star-struck or what? I wondered. Barely five minutes ago he had been sniveling over the perfidious Christine.

The man stepped forward, shook hands with both of us, and introduced himself as Auguste Talliere. He had the same dark brown hair and eyes and the same infectious smile as Tiffany.

"Everyone calls me Gus," he said, shrugging broad shoulders that were almost as magnificent as those of my erstwhile homicide detective friend. "I know what must be going through your mind: what were my parents thinking to give me a name like Auguste?" He smiled in a winsome, self-deprecating way, as if the name were his cross to bear for being born into a family whose roots stretched back to the antebellum period. "But it's a family name, the name Caesar gave his first born, my great-grandfather." He arched his brows comically as if to say *What's a fellow to do?*

"I notice you pronounce Caesar the French way, 'Say-czar.'"

"It is French. Caesar was originally from French Guiana," Gus said mildly. "Say-czar Talliere."

Tiffany rolled her eyes. "They don't want to hear about that ancient history stuff. They're here to see the house. Ashley's already been through it but Jon has not."

She took Jon by the hand and led him up the steps and onto the portico. I was paired off with Auguste—Gus.

"I hope you guys will agree to do this for us," Tiffany continued. "We know it's a disaster. But we hear you're the best and we want it to be perfect. Don't we Gus?" She tossed her big brother a winning smile as she pushed open the massive front door.

I caught Jon staring at her long, shapely legs. "I don't see why there'd be a problem," he said.

"Maybe you'd better wait until you see it," I said.

"Oh, you've got to say yes, Jon," Tiffany said, looking up at him and flirting madly.

Gus laughed. "My little sister's used to getting her way, Jon, but I'm with her all the way on this one. I think when you look the old homestead over and see the possibilities, you'll be as eager to do the job as we are to have you do it. Hurry up, little sister, the man hasn't got all day."

"Yes, let me give you the tour," Tiffany said.

She led us into the huge, formal reception hall. It ran from the front of the house straight through to the back. Pilasters separated the walls into panels, and transoms over doorways were decorated with classical motifs.

Four rooms opened off the center hall, two to a side. The back door stood open and through it I had a glimpse of the lake and the cypress gardens.

Against one long wall, a shabby sofa stood all alone. Shabby, but valuable. The real thing. There was no confusing those sweeping curves, or the dolphin motif that supported the arms, hand carved to resemble scales and tapered to form a flipped tail. The dolphin's snub-nosed head became the sofa's foot. It was high-style Empire from around 1820. And worth a fortune.

On the wall next to me, a family portrait hung. Underneath, mail was piled up on a table, along with an odd object that caused me to do a double take.

Gus saw me staring at it. "It's a sea turtle's skull," he said.

I examined it closely. It was as white as limestone, the eyes were large dark holes, and the nose-hole was set close to the eyes. There was no chin.

I felt a pang of sadness. I'm a member of the turtle watch on Wrightsville Beach. Guiding loggerhead hatchlings from the nest to the sea has brought me so much pleasure, I couldn't help wondering how this fully-grown sea turtle had met its end.

Gus pointed to the portrait above. "That's Caesar," he explained.

I'd seen the painting on an earlier visit but hadn't taken a good look. I did now and deciphered the signature of G.P.A. Healy, a follower of Thomas Sully, who'd traveled through the South in the late eighteen-hundreds to paint portraits of Southern men of distinction. Healy had portrayed Caesar as fierce and proud. His skin was light brown, his black hair short and crisp. He had full lips and his deep-set, hooded eyes were shrewd.

"And he was your great-grandfather?"

"He was my father's great-grandfather. My great-great-grandfather." Eyes that bore a strong resemblance to Caesar's looked out at me from Gus's face. "Caesar was brought to Wilmington as a slave when he was younger than Tiffany."

He watched for my reaction.

I said what I'd always heard my daddy, who was one of New Hanover County's best beloved judges, say, "Slavery was a great evil."

Gus's expression softened and I felt like I'd passed some litmus test with him. "The irony, Ashley, is that slavery was abolished in French Guiana in 1848, when Caesar was eight years old. He was free, but that meant nothing to the slave traders who shanghaied him ten years later. Caesar was ..."

"Come on, you two," Tiffany called from an adjoining room.

"You and Jon go on ahead. We'll catch up," Gus called back. Lowering his voice, he asked softly, "Or do you want to go with them, Ashley?"

"Not at all," I said, feeling as if he were casting a spell over me. "Please finish what you were saying."

"Caesar was captured and taken by force from his home, brought to this country in 1857. He was a very valuable commodity in this port city because of his skill as a river pilot, and he brought a good price for his captors. His new owner put him to work piloting the incoming trading vessels up the Cape Fear. It was dangerous work to pilot the ships over the treacherous shoals, but Caesar was fearless and as an Ndjuka Maroon was expert at boat building and navigating. Being out on the river afforded him a certain degree of freedom, so after a couple of years, he was able to escape to the blackwater swamps that used to surround this area. That's where he and other Maroons hid until Emancipation and the end of the war."

"What's a Maroon?" I asked.

"The word maroon comes from the Spanish word, *chimaroon*, which means fierce and wild. The former slaves of French Guiana and Suriname are known as Maroons, and the name was applied to the escaped slaves here who lived out in the swamps, far beyond the reach of slave-holders and their puppet lawmen."

"That's fascinating, Gus. But how do you know all this? Did Caesar," and I pronounced the name as he did, "keep a journal?"

Gus nodded. "Caesar could read and write in French and English; he was an exceptionally intelligent man. So, yes, he did keep a journal. It is one of the Talliere family's most cherished possessions, passed down from father to son. I own it now, although Beverly Tetterton would like me to donate it to the North Carolina Room at the library. I keep the original in a safe deposit box and I won't part with it. Not as long as I draw breath. I've had offers from publishers who want to publish it. Perhaps I will if the right offer comes along."

3

"The first thing we have to do," Jon was saying to Tiffany as they re-emerged from the double parlor, "is to repair the broken windows. I notice many have been boarded up, but rain's still getting in and damaging the floors and walls."

"The first thing . . . ! Then you'll do it! You'll restore the house for us." She flung her arms wide, gave Jon a hard hug, then stepped back. "I've seen the houses you've restored. I know the good work you guys do. Moon Gate is going to be grand again with you two restoring it!"

She moved close to Gus, wrapped her arms around his waist, and leaned her head on his shoulder. "They're going to do it for us, Gus. Didn't I tell you they would?"

Gus just shook his head indulgently. "She always gets her way."

"I like the name Moon Gate," I said. "My own house is known as the Reverend Israel Barton house, with a plaque and a pedigree. Houses are like people; they have personalities—and secrets."

"Caesar called it Moon Gate," Tiffany replied. "He wrote in his journal about how he'd installed the moon gates, then decided to name the house after them. Caesar traveled widely, and he was fascinated with English gardens. The landscape designer we hired to restore the terrace gardens educated me on the history of English gardens. During the 19th century, the English installed Chinese garden art in their own gardens, and the moon gate was a very popular feature."

Gus beamed, obviously proud of his young sister.

Tiffany's enthusiasm seemed boundless, and she went on, "The circle is a symbol of perfection to the Chinese."

"A moon-gate garden is a romantic place on a moonlit night," Gus added, his glance sweeping over me.

Is this guy coming on to me? I asked myself. That was a "no-no" if we were going work for him.

"So much for the magical," I said. "Now on to the practical. Jon, what's your assessment of the first floor?"

"Why don't we go upstairs and I'll save my evaluation until I've seen the whole house. I'm taking notes." He waved a notepad at me, as if to reassure me that while he might have been momentarily captivated by Tiffany's nubile charms, he was at heart a serious architect who wasn't being diverted from the job at hand.

Good old Jon. I smiled inwardly. "Okay, let's take this show upstairs then. There's some water damage there, I'm afraid."

I paused at the newel post, and pointed to the handrail. "Anybody know the significance of this gold coin?"

"What coin?" Tiffany asked, stepping up behind me and peering where I pointed. "Oh, that old thing. That's been there for as long as I can remember. I didn't know it had a special meaning. I just thought it was one of Caesar's eccentricities."

Gus stifled a grin. He knew. I turned to Jon and arched my eyebrows inquiringly. He leaned in closer for a better look. A gold coin had been imbedded in the wood at the center of the handrail where it crowned the newel post. Jon shrugged his shoulders. "Beats me."

I smiled. "That gold coin was set there to signify that the house was owned free and clear by Caesar, that all debts had been paid, that there were no liens, and any visitor to the house who saw that coin knew the owner of the house was a man of substance. Probably, he gave a formal party and they celebrated at the time. That was the tradition back then."

Jon rolled his eyes. "She knows all the old-house trivia."

"That's my job," I said with a chuckle. That gold coin must have been a temptation to the poor Tallieres, yet somehow they'd resisted the urge to pry it lose and spend it. They had hung on to this symbol of their proud heritage, and I admired them for it.

We started up the stairs which were in surprisingly good condition. Stairs generally hold up better than other parts of a structure. On the second floor, the water damage was obvious.

"We're going to need to do some extensive roof repair," Jon said, studying the sepia stains that tinged the ceiling and upper walls of a sparsely furnished bedroom.

Throughout the house, only a few furnishings remained, and it was my guess that Caesar's descendants had been forced to sell off valuable antiques to get them through hard times. I was grateful that they'd had the fortitude to hold on to the house and land. Surely there had been offers over the years.

Jon continued, "I'd say past storms have loosened or blown away some of the slate tiles. But we've got someone good who'll be able to make the repairs and replace the slate."

"Willie Hudson," I said. "A very experienced contractor who knows more about old house construction than Jon and I put together."

"We'll leave the subcontracting to you," Gus said. "Jon, have you noticed how the floor sags under some of those windows?"

"I have. The paint has peeled off the window frames, allowing rot to set in. Let the bottom sill rot out and the whole house starts to sink, roof and all. Most people aren't aware of just how important window sills are to a house's overall structural integrity. And all it takes is regular painting to prevent water damage."

Tiffany's enthusiasm waned. I could see this was getting too technical for her. She just wanted her house to look pretty again, she didn't want to know how we were going to do it. "Unfortunately, there hasn't been the money to maintain the house until recently. All we had was our good name."

"We'll come back tomorrow and make a detailed inspection," I assured her. "We'll take photographs and measurements, and draw up a comprehensive plan. Then we'll be able to tell you how much this will cost."

Tiffany waved a hand dismissively. "Money's not a problem. We've both done well. We've been very lucky, I with my acting, Gus with his investments."

"You are eligible for tax credits with this type restoration. I'll prepare the necessary applications for you," I said.

"Well, that's great, Ashley. Still, we can't start tomorrow. The Azalea Queen's coronation is scheduled for the morning, and our producer is insisting we all be there. A photo op that can't be missed, he says.

"Then in the afternoon, Gus and I are hosting a garden party here for the queen's court and the festival officials. Your sister Melanie as the grand marshal will be here, and we'd like you and Jon to be our special guests. Will you come?"

Jon and I exchanged looks, nodded, and I accepted for both of us. "We'd love to come. We can inspect the house on Monday after the festival is over."

"That's great. Come on, let me show you our quarters. There's an enclosed porch where you and Jon can set up an office if you want."

Tiffany and Gus proceeded us down the stairs, across a piazza, and into the north wing of the house. Here, with the addition of electricity, plumbing, and carpentry, the wing's first floor had been converted into a liveable apartment. There were two bedrooms, two bathrooms, a sitting room with a Pullman kitchen, and an odd little room that appeared to be an enclosed service porch.

Tiffany and Gus shared the apartment after he'd finished his studies at Duke, she'd told me on my first visit. Having him return to Moon Gate meant she could return too; the place was just too forbidding for a twenty-year-old to live here on her own. When Gus granted himself the present of a long trip through South America, Tiffany had stayed at a downtown Bed and Breakfast. Now they were sharing again, and Tiffany seemed happy with the arrangement.

Indicating the enclosed porch, Tiffany said, "This is the room I was talking about." She hooked her hair behind her ear with an index finger in the signature mannerism she'd perfected for her role as Julie on *Dolphin's Cove.*

As we passed through the first floor rooms again, I spotted more displays of animal skulls on shelves and tabletops. One in particular caught my eye. It was large and bleached white like the skulls one sees in Georgia O'Keefe's desert paintings. The jaw was long and narrow, and at first I mistook it for a horse's head. Then I realized it was a pelican skull, and I thought these were odd items to collect. I wondered if they'd been acquired recently, or were they prizes from a distant Talliere's collection?

4

Thursday dawned gloriously, one of those incredibly beautiful days that are rare and remain indelibly imprinted on the brain as the epitome of a perfect spring day. During the night, a gentle rain had washed away pollen and dust and refreshed the flowers. The colorful azaleas stood out vividly against a stark white tent that had been set-up on the lawn between the Talliere mansion and Caesar's terraced gardens.

Groups of Azalea Belles in pastel ballgowns strolled the lawns, parasols raised to shield fair faces, and they smiled and giggled with the princess and her court. The princess this year was a high school senior from Hoggard, bright and possessing a promising future.

I had been concerned that the crumbling mansion would appear inappropriate as a backdrop for the festivities, but I needn't have worried. The house came across as a faded Tara, much the way Scarlett's home had appeared when she returned to it after the war, and thus endearing itself to the heart and soul of any Southerner.

As the kitchen was unusable, the caterer was operating out of the tent. Her van was parked on the far side, and I recognized it as belonging to Elaine McDuff. Elaine was a round, motherly-looking, energetic forty-something caterer. Larry, her husband, was a sometime character actor, who as a young man had been a regular on the *Matlock* series

when it was filmed here in Wilmington. Since th
been hard to come by and he seemed to have sett
with her popular catering business.

The flaps of the tent were rolled up. Inside, Elaine
buffet tables with pristine white cloths for the food she was setting out.

Round tables and wrought iron garden chairs had been placed strategically in shady spots on the lawn for the guests. There were lounge chairs under the trees and my sister Melanie reclined in one. As the festival's grand marshal, she would lead the parade and preside over many of the ceremonies in the days to come. Melanie is famous for her spectacular beauty and her spectacular success as a Wilmington realtor.

Next to her sat the Azalea Queen, Jillian Oliver, a stunning platinum blonde, gorgeous in her own right, but no match for my red-headed sister who, in her spring green sequined sheath, looked smashing. Jillian, a star on a big network soap opera that was filmed in New York, chatted companionably with Melanie.

"Looks like prom night out there," Jon said over my shoulder.

"Not these days," I replied. "Today the seventeen-year-olds wear slinky black gowns on prom night and no one would ever accuse them of being virgins. No, these girls look like true Southern belles."

Melanie beckoned to me but I raised a just-a-minute finger. I was looking around for Tiffany to tell her we had arrived. I spotted her in the tent, hovering over the tables. Elaine had returned to the van, unloading food boxes onto the tailgate, while Larry was doing a balancing-act with a tray of iced tea glasses as he moved through the crowd.

"I'm going to speak to Tiffany," I told Jon.

"And I see a city councilman I need to speak to," he replied, and walked toward a group of men that included Gus Talliere. Gus gave me a little salute.

I'd dressed up for the party. Although I wouldn't be mistaken for of the Azalea Belles, in my ankle-length silky tea gown and feminine straw hat with flowers, I thought I could hold my own against any belle of the Twelve Oaks variety.

I exchanged waves with several acquaintances then made my way to the tent where I called to Tiffany. I must have startled her for she whirled around awkwardly, hand pressed to heart. “Oh, Ashley, I didn’t hear you.”

I gave her a little hug. “I wanted to let you know we’re here. Everything looks so pretty.”

“Do you really think so? I’m a bit nervous, that’s why I’m in here checking on things.”

“I do think so. It’s a beautiful party and a beautiful day. Don’t worry about the food, there’s no finer chef than Elaine. Just leave everything in her capable hands and come on out and enjoy yourself. By the way, you look fabulous.”

Tiffany looked like a fairytale princess in her pale yellow gown with its full skirt. Her hair was swept up, and unlike yesterday, she was wearing make-up.

“Come on,” I said, my arm around her shoulders, “Melanie’s been motioning for me to get over there, and my sister is ‘she who cannot be denied.’”

Laughing together, we strolled across the grass to Melanie and Queen Jillian.

“You took long enough,” Melanie scolded. “Ashley, this is Jillian Oliver, our queen, and a most talented actress. Jillian, my baby sister, Ashley.”

Jillian smiled graciously and extended her hand. “Ashley, I’m pleased to meet you. And hi, again, Tiffany. You’re so sweet to give this party for us. Now, Ashley, Melanie has been telling me all about your living in New York and studying at Parsons. Do you miss the big city?”

"Not really. I loved New York when I lived there, and I go back to visit friends." My college roommate and her brother live in New York and we see each other often. "And catch up on Broadway plays. But this is home; I'm happy here."

"Ashley, Melanie, I just love your names. We don't have such romantic names in my family. But this is a most romantic place. I've never been to Wilmington before but now that I'm here, I just adore it. How lucky you are to live in this garden paradise."

"Thanks," I said, rather surprised that a big star could be so nice.

Mindy Chesterton, who had the leading role on *Dolphin's Cove*, flounced over to us, flicked her scarf at a lounge chair to dislodge imaginary dust, then settled into it. Mindy was buxom in her pink satin gown that fit like a second skin.

"I can't wait till this tacky festival is over," she complained. "Whatever made Cameron think having the cast participate in the Azalea Festival would be good publicity for the show?"

Cameron Jordan was the executive producer of *Dolphin's Cove* and the president of Gem Star Pictures which he founded. He was also Melanie's current *amour*.

I turned to Tiffany and lifted my eyebrows, as if to inquire, *What's eating her*?

Tiffany made a slight shrug. *Don't ask me.*

Melanie, who doesn't take anything from anybody, said, "Cam knows what he's doing."

Tiffany interceded, making peace, "Mindy, you know Ashley, don't you? She's Melanie's younger sister."

"Of course I know Ashley. In Wilmington, people from good families all know each other."

Was that a put down? A slight because Tiffany was descended from a slave?

Mindy gave some passing belles a haughty stare. "I used to have to dress up like that when I was a belle. Ya'll know what they've got on under those ballgowns? Hoops and pantaloons. A bustle. The whole outfit must weigh ten pounds." She leered. "Know what I've got on under this gown?"

When no one replied, she said, "Not much."

She arched her back and fanned a bee away with her hand.

"But they look so pretty," Jillian said. "So . . . antebellum."

"Antebellum, antiquated," Mindy complained. "My mother pushed me into being a belle when I was a teenager. Thank goodness I got too old for it."

"But being a belle is your family's tradition," Melanie said. "Why, I remember seeing your mother riding on a float in the parade when I was a little girl. She was the prettiest thing you ever saw in that gorgeous pink ballgown."

"That was my grandmother's dress. Mama wore it and I wore it too. Grandmama was one of the first belles, back in the fifties," she added.

Despite her complaints, Mindy seemed to take pride in her family's close association with the festival which began as a dream for Dr. Houston Moore in 1948.

"Well, it's a sweet tradition," Jillian said.

"My family have been in society since the war," Mindy boasted.

Jillian's expression turned puzzled. "World War II?"

Mindy rolled her eyes, sighing audibly. "No, the War Between the States. Don't you know anything?"

Jillian uttered a soft *oh* and flushed deeply. It had to be a stressful day for her, yet she was the soul of courtesy. Early that morning, she'd boarded the Henrietta III at the State Port, ferried upriver to the waterfront for her coronation ceremony at Riverfront Park. She was probably tired of smiling and waving and making nice, yet she rallied on, every word that left her lips was pleasant.

Unlike rude Mindy. How she'd ever landed the starring role on *Dolphin's Cove* was beyond me.

Reclaiming her dignity, Jillian said to Melanie, "The organizers of this festival do a superb job."

"Our mama used to be a volunteer when we were little," Melanie replied. "She took us to all the events."

I looked from Mindy to Tiffany, both actresses on *Dolphin's Cove*. Mindy was the exact opposite of Tiffany. Her yellow blonde straight hair was pulled up in a pony tail. Tiffany's dark hair tended to frizz the way mine did. Mindy's eyes were china blue; Tiffany's chocolate brown. Tiffany seemed to have been born with a sunny disposition; Mindy was sulky, and tended to whine.

Mindy gave Jillian an appraising look, then said, "Can I try on the crown?"

"What?" Jillian asked, taken aback. The rest of us gasped.

Mindy pouted. "Well, in all the years I served at these festivals, I never did get to wear the crown. I'd like to see how it looks on me."

Jillian laughed lightly. "I hope I'm not breaking any rules, but here, take it."

She reached up and lifted the crown off her head. It was covered with Austrian crystals. Gingerly, she handed it to Mindy.

Must be heavy, I thought.

We all watched, breathless, as Mindy "crowned" herself.

"Quick, someone, hand me a mirror," she squealed.

Melanie dug in the purse beside her chair and passed a mirror to Mindy. Catching my eye, she arched an eyebrow. I'd hear about this later.

"You look beautiful," Jillian said sweetly.

Around us, heads turned and conversation stopped.

"I don't think you should be doing that," Tiffany commented.

"Oh, pooh, you are such a little goody two-shoes," Mindy told Tiffany.

Tiffany's mouth opened, but she bit back a retort. Instead she announced to Melanie and Jillian, "Ashley's going to restore Moon Gate for Gus and me."

"How nice," Jillian said.

"Good choice," Melanie commented. To Jillian, she said, "Ashley and her associate Jon are the best restorers around."

Mindy said nothing, just cast a critical gaze over the crumbling mansion. Her look was sour, like milk that had sat out in the sun and curdled.

"My daddy used to say he was going to buy Moon Gate for me," she said, "but he never did. Now that I've got money of my own, I just might buy it myself."

"Moon Gate is not for sale," Tiffany said firmly. There was a sharp edge to her voice I'd never heard before.

Good for her, I thought. She's got backbone.

Larry arrived with a tray of refreshments. Tiffany and I moved aside so he could set the tray down on a wicker table. He handed out tall, frosty glasses of iced tea. Each glass was garnished with a sprig of mint.

All around us, beverages were being eagerly consumed for the afternoon had turned hot with the sun beating down and moist air wafting off the Cape Fear.

We each took a glass of iced tea and thanked him.

"Enjoy," he said, hoisting the tray onto his shoulder and moving toward the next group.

Jillian sipped deeply. "My, that's good. I was parched."

Mindy took a sip, frowned, then set her glass down on the table with a thunk. "That tea's got sugar in it. I avoid sugar."

Melanie, who had drained half of her beverage in one swallow, gulped and said, "You're so wise. A teaspoon of sugar goes straight to my hips."

That was a lie. No matter what Melanie eats or drinks, she never gains an ounce.

Tiffany picked up Mindy's glass. "I'll take this back to the tent and bring you fresh unsweetened tea. Or do you want *Sweet'n'Low*?"

"No artificial sweeteners. Don't you know they cause cancer?"

Tiffany headed toward the tent, her long skirt floating over the grass. She was vivacious and friendly, and in my opinion would make a better star of *Dolphin's Cove* than Mindy.

Melanie was trying to sell Jillian a beach house. She described an "absolutely gorgeous, perfect-for-entertaining house" on Wrightsville Beach, as Jillian nodded her bare head.

"And if you ever decide to buy something grander, Mindy," Melanie said, "Now's the time. The mortgage rate has bottomed out; it's a buyer's market."

Melanie had sold Mindy a lovely house at Landfall when Mindy started to earn major bucks and had decided it was time to move out of her parents' Forest Hills home.

But Mindy didn't reply, was staring into the distance with narrowed eyes. I followed her gaze into the tent as the curdled-milk expression crossed her face again. Jimmy Ryder, her co-star, stood at one of the buffet tables, deep in conversation with Tiffany. Heather Thorp and Brook Cole, the two other females in the cast, stood off to one side, heads together, eyeing Jimmy and Tiffany.

I wondered if one of the festival officials would come running over and demand that Jillian's crown be restored to her queenly head. Mindy showed no sign of giving it up. I caught sight of Jon button-holing the city councilman who looked like he wanted to bolt, and gave him a little wave.

Tiffany had left Jimmy and was now mingling with her guests.

Mindy grumbled, "What's keeping that girl?" as if referring to a servant. "I'm dying of thirst."

Inside the tent the guests were lined up at the buffet tables, filling plates with Elaine's specialties. I recognized cast members of *Dolphin's Cove*, festival officials, and the mayor.

Eventually, Tiffany returned, bearing a small tray with a tall glass of iced tea. Graciously, she handed the glass and a napkin to Mindy with a smile. "Not a drop of sugar. Elaine guarantees it."

The glass was garnished with the obligatory mint sprig.

Mindy took the glass without so much as a thank-you, and with one hand holding the crown in place, tilted her head back and gulped it down. She made a face, complaining, "My, that's bitter. I don't why everyone raves about Elaine's culinary skills. Why, she almost gave me ptomaine once."

I wondered why Mindy treated Tiffany, and everyone, so shamefully. And now she was badmouthing Elaine. Granted Mindy was a star, but surely her society mother and grandmother had taught her better manners.

Disgusted with her attitude, I turned my back on her and said to Tiffany, "I'd like to do a complete inventory of the furniture that's left, and the paintings, then send the stuff out to refinishers while we've got the house torn up. I want to incorporate the original antiques in our . . ."

Interrupted by a strange gurgling sound, I turned to see the glass fall from Mindy's hand. She was clutching her stomach and gasping for air as the gurgling sound bubbled up from her throat. Jerky spasms convulsed her body, then it went rigid.

I rushed to her side and knelt down beside her.

Melanie jumped up and yelled, "A doctor! We need a doctor! Someone call an ambulance!"

We all looked helplessly down on an unconscious Mindy. The jeweled crown lay upsidedown in the grass next to the overturned glass and Mindy's purse.

Several people pulled out cell phones and dialed 911. Tiffany ran inside the house and returned with a blanket which she tucked around Mindy's stone-still body.

We stood about, not knowing what to do, shocked, whispering. "It was a bee," Melanie declared. "There was a swarm of them. I think one stung her. She must be allergic."

I reached down and lifted Mindy's purse. "Maybe's she's got one of those antivenin kits in here." I opened the purse but there wasn't much in it. Lipstick, a couple of twenties, and a key ring.

"No antivenin kit," I said.

But by then we heard the ambulance's siren, growing louder and louder.

5

Driving with Melanie is not for the faint of heart.

"Slow down," I yelled, bracing my foot against the floorboard as if to stop the car with a non-existent brake. "You're going to get us killed." But Melanie's green satin pump only pressed more firmly on the accelerator.

"We've got to keep up with the ambulance," she replied.

Melanie always drives fast. She could beat Kyle Petty in a Nascar race if she had a mind to. She'd given up her Lexus SUV, complaining that she could get more speed out of a camel in the desert. The sleek new Jaguar XKR convertible she'd replaced the SUV with was finished in Jupiter Red with a black convertible top. Inside, the cabin was wood and leather. All very plush, very expensive, very real.

We tore up Carolina Beach Road after the ambulance, on our way to New Hanover Regional Medical Center.

Nearing an intersection, Melanie bent into the steering wheel and leaned on the horn, intent on making it through, whether the light was with us or not.

"That was a red light!" I screeched.

"We're with an emergency vehicle. They have to stop for us," she declared with assurance.

"We're . . . ? Oh, I give up. Just be careful. Why are we doing this anyway? It's not like Mindy's a friend."

Melanie gave me a look, mouth turned down.

"Watch the road!" I shouted as we just barely missed side-swiping an old Caddy. Those things are built like tanks.

"You know, you can be so callous sometimes," Melanie complained. "Aren't you the least little bit concerned about poor Mindy's fate? Why, we were right there when it happened. The doctors might need to know what we saw."

"I didn't see anything," I said, then reacted predictably with a sharp pang of guilt. Melanie knows how to push my buttons, and she'd scored a direct hit. I didn't like Mindy, and although I tried to conceal my feelings, Melanie can always see through me.

"Cam had the presence of mind to call Janet and Nem Chesterton, Mindy's parents; they'll be there when we arrive. Nem's one of the show's investors."

Cameron Jordan, the president of Gem Star Pictures, was responsible for the overnight sensation, *Dolphin's Cove.* After L.A. and New York, Wilmington ranks third in the nation for the production of movies—and television shows, like the long running *Matlock* series, which was produced and filmed here as well.

"Poor dears," Melanie continued. "Imagine, seeing your only daughter being wheeled in on a stretcher."

"Well, because of Nem Chesterton, Wilmington will be a war zone this fall. He announced this morning that he's running for mayor in the next mayoralty election."

"And you object to that because . . . ? " Melanie asked in the infuriating older-sister condescending tone she sometimes uses with me.

"M—e—l," I cried indignantly as if the answer was obvious. "There can't be a more divisive candidate than Nem Chesterton. With him running things, I pity the fate of the historic district. Surely, he hasn't got a chance."

"You never know," she said. "There are many who share his views."

"Oh? And are you one of them?"

Nehemiah Chesterton was a rich and powerful attorney-slash-developer who claimed to be descended from one of Wilmington's founding families.

"You know how I feel, Ashley. I adore the historic district. Some of my best sales involve those old houses. Young people and retirees like to buy them and fix them up. And where would the movie industry be if they couldn't come here and film our historic district, as well as our coastal areas?"

She continued, "And Nem Chesterton will be good for business. Why do the two have to be mutually exclusive?"

"I don't know why," I confessed. "They just are. The 'pro-business' interests always want to condemn old structures, raze them, and build parking decks."

"Well, we do have a parking problem downtown," Melanie said in a reasonable voice that only frustrated me more.

"Well," I argued back, "instead of building more parking decks, we ought to be looking for ways to reduce traffic."

She cast me a cynical eye. "That'd be the day. Americans have a love affair with their cars. Just look at you and me; you love your Alero, I love this sweet thing." For emphasis she stepped down on the accelerator and the powerful car shot forward.

"Slow down! What I mean is, why can't we find ways to leave our cars at home? The beauty of living downtown is that we can walk everywhere, with the exception of a first-class grocery store. Wouldn't it be a smart move to persuade one of those fresh-produce-type folks to renovate a storefront on Market Street and install a fabulous grocery store?"

"A very smart move. Why don't you run for mayor?"

I snorted derisively. "I've got all the work I can handle, thank you very much. Anyway politics is a dirty business."

"Well, maybe I'll run. I'm a born leader and I don't mind getting my hands dirty if the outcome is a good one."

Coming from anyone else, this type of assertion would have been obnoxious. But with Melanie, the statement was so true, no one could take offense.

Ahead, the ambulance stopped at the ER entrance, the siren dying abruptly like an injured animal put out of its misery. Melanie pulled up short directly behind the ambulance. The back doors opened from inside and an EMT jumped down as the driver raced around from the cab. Together they lowered Mindy's stretcher to the ground and did something to it so that it sprang up on legs. Then they ran with it through the automatic doors.

Melanie started to open her car door when a rotund security guard trotted up to the Jag.

"Ma'am, you can't park here," he said between breaths. "You gotta pull round into the parking lot. Plenty spaces there."

"But, Captain," Melanie said, batting her eyelashes at him, "that was our sister in that ambulance. She's dreadfully ill. We've got to be with her."

Sister?

"Look, ma'am, you ain't gonna be able to go back where they're takin' your sister anyways. So, you just go on now and park this nice car over yonder. I'll meet you at the door and personally show you to the nurses' station." He smiled down at her. "Ain't you got yourself a sweet piece of machinery, ma'am?"

"Oh, all right," Melanie said sullenly and peeled off, wheels squealing, almost clipping the guard's pointing arm.

We skidded into a slot not more than thirty feet from the entrance,

Melanie frowning all the while. "Give a man a uniform and he becomes a little dictator."

Inside the hospital, I thanked the guard for showing us to the nurses' station. We could have wandered around for hours trying to find it ourselves. You need a road map inside medical facilities these days.

Janet Chesterton was sitting on the edge of her chair as Nem paced the corridor. Janet jumped up when she saw us and Nem hurried over.

"What happened to her?" Janet cried. "They won't tell us anything."

"We don't know, Janet," Melanie said kindly. She put her arm around Janet's shaking shoulders. "But Ashley saw it all."

Janet turned to me, eyes beseeching. "What happened to my baby, Ashley?"

Nem hovered, looking like he wanted to join in all the hugging but was afraid it might ruin his reputation if someone saw him.

"I honestly don't know, Janet. One minute she was fine, the next she was shaking and gasping. Is she allergic to bees? There was a swarm of them around the flowers."

"Bees?" Janet said vaguely. She turned to Nem. "Bees? A bee did this to my little girl?"

"Mindy is not allergic to bees," Nem said emphatically. "No, it's got to be something else. What about toxic shock syndrome? I've been hearing a lot about that lately."

I shook my head. "Why don't you all sit down. You'll feel better. Would you like some coffee? I'll go get some for you."

Janet and Nem settled wearily in the hard molded-plastic chairs.

"Oh," I said, "I almost forgot. Here. It's Mindy's purse."

I handed the small pink satin purse to Janet. She opened it and looked inside. Snapped it closed. She had a vacant look about her, like she was someplace else.

Then she seemed to come to. Handing the purse back to me, she said, "Take care of this for me, Ashley, will you? Her house keys are inside. Would you drive out to Landfall and pack some of her personal things in an overnight bag and bring them here. She'll need nice things when she wakes up."

Janet seemed to think Mindy was going to wake up, like she was taking an unscheduled nap. I guess I would have seen it that way in her place.

"Sure, I'll be glad to. What shall I bring?"

"You're such a sweet girl, Ashley," Janet said vaguely. "Mindy always said that about you."

I knew this wasn't true. Mindy didn't say nice things about anybody.

Janet looked around for moment, like she had forgotten what she was saying. "Oh, yes. Bring. Hair brush, toothbrush and tooth paste, a pretty nightgown and robe. Slippers. Mindy will be mortified when she wakes up in one of those nasty hospital gowns. She's always so particular about her appearance."

"Excuse us a minute," Melanie said, dragging me off to one side, out of earshot. Glancing up at the industrial-size hospital clock, she said, "I've got to be downtown at five to do the ribbon-cutting at the art show. And you've got to go with me. Then I'll drop you at your house so you can get your car and get on with your mercy mission."

I walked back to Janet and Nem. "It'll take me about an hour. Would you call the gate at Landfall and instruct the guard to let me in. You know how security conscious they are out there. Now, don't worry. Mindy's going to be fine. The doctors here are wonderful."

"Thank you, Ashley," Janet said. Nem seemed struck mute, like the situation was too much for him, a crisis best left to women. "You always were such a sweet girl," Janet repeated.

Toting Mindy's purse, I scurried after Melanie out of the hospital and out to her car. "Now see what you've done," I said. Which, typically, is her line to me.

6

The Wilmington Art Association was holding its Annual Spring Art Show and Sale at St. Thomas Preservation Hall on Dock Street. Melanie smiled into the cameras, then snipped the ribbon. I don't believe she'd ever cut a ribbon before but she performed the ceremonial act as graciously as the Azalea Queen herself. The art show, with 150 artists presenting, was now officially open.

Cameron moved to Melanie's side, an ever present hand pressed lightly to her back or on her arm. The sign of ownership. *I can touch her but you cannot*, was the message this gesture was supposed to convey to other men.

I liked Cameron. He was good for Melanie. He'd moved to Wilmington from Los Angeles where he'd been the executive vice president for programming at HBO. He'd wanted out, he told us, wanted his own production company, and he built it. Now, with a big success on his hands, he deserved all the rewards.

Together, Melanie and I filled him in on Mindy's arrival at the hospital, how shaken Janet and Nem had been, and even Janet's request that I collect Mindy's things from her home.

I dangled the purse. "Mindy's. I've got her keys."

We speculated about what might have happened to her. "Well,

whatever it is," he said, "we're shooting bright and early in the morning so if she can't make it, I've got to alert the writers to write her out, revise the scenes, give Tiffany a larger role."

Business came first, and show biz came first, last, and always.

"Well, Nem will know. Call him," Melanie advised. "Later."

"Just between us, I wouldn't be unhappy to write her out for good. She's a prima donna. And poison on the set."

Why did you give her the part? I wanted to ask. Then, in a flash I knew. Nem Chesterton had been an investor early on, when most people doubted that a show about a group of high school seniors could make it. Now, Cameron had his choice of investors, beating them away with a stick, no doubt.

Cameron confirmed this with, "I don't need Nem's money now. I'd sure like to be rid of Mindy though. Tiffany's the one I'd like to see in the major role. That little girl is dynamite."

I've noticed that men tend to blab freely when they are trying to impress a woman. And Cameron was clearly trying to impress Melanie. In fact, he was star-struck where she was concerned.

"Well, come on now, sweet cakes, no more talk of business," she cooed up at him. "Let's look at all these pretty pictures, and forget about those worrisome details for a while."

Melanie wandered to the displays of colorful original works of art.

"Now, look at this," she said. "Oh, I do love this one."

The picture was executed in oil on a large canvas, with splashes of brilliant color, a scene that might have been painted on Wrightsville Beach. The south end of the beach at sunset perhaps, the sky layered in reds and pinks, the sun setting in the west just outside the frame, shooting rods of flame over the sand dunes.

"Beautiful," Melanie sighed.

I looked at the two of them. In a world of their own, shoulders touching, body language saying, *we're a couple*. Cameron adored her, I saw that the first time I met him. And well he should. My sister might exasperate me, but she's very special. Stunningly beautiful, smart, hard-working, and at the top of her profession. And my cat loved her too. Animals never misjudge character the way we humans do.

I joined them in front of the oil painting. It was breathtaking. "That'd look great in your living room, Mel," I told her, "over the fireplace. You sometimes have a view like that from your sliding glass doors."

Her mouth turned petulant. "Oh, but look. It's sold."

A large sold sign hung from the frame.

"What a shame," Cameron said coyly.

Melanie gave him an appraising look. She leaned in and peered at the sold sign. Then she squealed and threw her arms around his neck. "You devil. You bought it. I can't believe you."

He kissed her cheeks and hugged her hard. "I knew you'd love it. Don't you have a birthday coming up soon?"

"No, not till August. You know I'm a Leo."

"Well, then, let's just say it's my gift to the most dazzling creature in the world for putting up with an old geezer like me."

She smacked his arm playfully. "Stop that. And thank you, darlin'." She kissed him on the mouth, not caring who saw or what they thought.

Will that ever happen to me? I wondered wistfully. Nick was back in town and hadn't even called.

7

I walked the few blocks to my house and got into my baby blue Alero. Then I drove out Oleander to Eastwood Road. At six o'clock, the early evening was pleasant and I powered down the windows, sensing the ocean's presence as I drove nearer to Landfall. The posh, walled community had been developed on the former estate of the wealthy Pembroke Joneses who'd once hosted lavish parties there and at their Newport mansion. They'd been two of Mrs. Astor's four hundred. When people talk about "keeping up with the Joneses," it's Pembroke and Sarah they're referring to.

I showed the gatehouse guard my driver's license and he informed me officiously that he had received instructions from Mr. Nehemiah Chesterton to admit me, just this once.

I wound around the circular roadways within the complex, past a rolling greensward of the Jack Nicklaus golf course, then the Frank H. Kenan Chapel. Everywhere, there was an abundance of flowering azaleas and dogwoods, and in the distance, breath-taking vistas of the Intracoastal Waterway.

Finally I reached Mindy's house which was a large residence in the transitional style so popular just now, faced with some sort of fake limestone and having a great many Palladian windows. Inside, there'd be a two-story foyer and great room and a sense of spaciousness.

I parked out front, went up the sidewalk and using the keys from the pink satin purse, let myself in the front door. Inside, I paused to get my bearings. The house had that spooky silence houses get when they're empty.

The interior was beautiful and, as I'd been informed by Melanie, had been professionally decorated by the design firm of Belinda Bell Art & Accessories. I have a B.A. from Parsons in interior design myself and an M.F.A. in historic preservation from SCAD, the Savannah College of Art and Design.

Still, if some institution ever granted degrees in snooping, I'd have one, *magna cum laude*. Here I was alone in pouty Mindy's home, and with a legal right to be here. What an excellent opportunity to satisfy my insatiable curiosity!

On my left was the dining room with its sponged gold walls and ivory trim. The floor was hardwood and the Persian rug under the dining room table and chairs was rich with smoky browns, golds, reds and corals. I strolled in to stroke the satiny, waxed table top. Good furniture, Sheraton, the real thing. *Okay, Wilkes, stop admiring the antiques*!

The foyer's ceiling soared to the rooftop. A Palladian window set above the front door admitted thin, evening light. On my right was the great room. There too the walls rose to the roof. The upstairs hallway overhung the great room like a balcony. The decor was opulent with cascading, fringed taffeta draperies and deeply padded furniture. Yet inviting. A plush ivory carpet covered the floor.

From the dining room, I entered the kitchen. I snapped on lights and inspected it too. The cabinets were made of a bleached birch, and there was one of those fancy temperature-controlled wine refrigerators. To my right, a sunroom ran the width of the house and I walked its length back to a rear hallway that connected to the foyer—ring-around-a-rosy.

In the master suite, I tapped a light switch just inside the door, causing all the lamps to blaze at once. Here, everything was soft in pale golds and greens, very pretty and feminine, but also in a frenzy so that I couldn't see the top of the bed for all the gowns heaped upon it. Evidently, Mindy had tried on several garments before selecting the pink satin gown. The rejected dresses puffed up on the bed like a multicolored parachute someone had discarded. A body could be hidden under all that silk and lace and I'd never know it.

Now why had I thought that? Maybe because it's a little spooky in here, I reasoned, and I'm all alone in another person's house—a person who is lying helpless in the hospital, unable to prevent me from prowling around her bedroom.

From the top shelf of a closet—there were two and they were huge and I couldn't help comparing them to the tiny, old fashioned closets in my house and feeling deprived—I pulled down an overnight bag.

In the bathroom I loaded the case with toiletry items, hair brush, toothbrush, perfume, all the things I thought Mindy might like to have when she awoke.

I found a pretty nightgown and robe on a silk-padded hanger and zipped them into a garment bag. Now where were her slippers?

Family pictures in antique silver frames covered most of the available surfaces in the room. Above the bed hung an ornately framed portrait of Mindy that must have been painted when she made her debut.

There were pictures of Janet and Nem, and their sons, Hugh and Nehemiah the Fourth, and pictures of the family as a whole, all five of them. Mindy was the little princess, the cherished baby sister. And in other snapshots, the Chesterton boys with their cousins. And a photo of Mindy with Jimmy Ryder, their arms wrapped around each other, an ocean behind them that was too blue to be the Atlantic. The Caribbean?

Slippers, I reminded myself. I looked around the room, finally spotting a pair of white silk ballet slippers under Mindy's desk. She must have toed them off when she'd been sitting at the computer.

It was turned on, humming, calling me to it like a siren's song. Mindy had not exited out of the program she'd been using earlier. Living alone, there was no need to hide anything.

I pulled out the chair and faced the screen. Quicken. I use it for my own accounts.

The colorful screen seemed to invite, *scroll me, please*, and as it asked nicely, I complied.

Mindy, who had always seemed like such an airhead to me, apparently managed her own money. I couldn't help being impressed. How often do we hear of actors and actresses who turn their large salaries over to financial managers, only to be ripped off and left destitute.

Wow! The deposits to Mindy's account were enormous. I knew actors made a bundle, but seeing those healthy monthly deposits made me wonder if I had chosen the wrong profession, if I ought not enroll in an acting class. Flipping through the pages, I learned that Mindy paid her bills on the first and the fifteenth. Mortgage and utilities on the first. Credit cards on the fifteenth.

She'd also withdrawn twenty thousand dollars in cash on the first of April. I scrolled back. There were identical entries on the first of every month. Cash. Twenty thousand. What had that been for? And why cash? How had she carried it around? Or did she? Maybe she was paying it to someone who didn't want a record of the transaction. But who? And why?

The telephone rang somewhere in the house, and Mindy's answering machine intercepted, her seductive voice inviting the caller to leave a message.

Suddenly, I felt uncomfortable, my conscience warning me this was private stuff and none of my business.

I knelt down and squeezed under the desk to retrieve the slippers. Smacking my head hard on the underside of the desk, I let out a yelp. Then, pulling away, something caught my hair and held it fast. What in the world?

I reached up and released several strands of hair from something sticky. Kneeling lower and peering up under the desk, I saw that a loose piece of duct tape had grabbed my hair. The duct tape was holding a padded envelope to the underside of the desk.

Jeez Louise, why'd I have to see that? I thought as I rubbed my sore head. Now what was I going to do? This was truly a moral dilemma. Open the envelope and see what was inside, or forever wonder what was so secret that Mindy had been forced to conceal the contents under the desk in her own house where she lived alone.

"No, no, no," I said aloud, my voice shattering the stillness. I am not going to pry further. Up and out. Grab the garment bag, grab the overnight case, and better take Mindy's purse too. I needed the keys to lock up after myself.

Later that night, after I had played at being "sweet, little Ashley" for Janet and had delivered Mindy's stuff to her waiting arms, and after I'd learned that there'd been no change in her condition, a rivetting idea shocked me out of a sound sleep.

Eyes wide open, I whispered to myself, "Mindy's being blackmailed." That's what those cash withdrawals were all about. And that's why she'd taped something to the bottom of her desk!

And subconsciously I must have known this all along for why else had I failed to return Mindy's pink satin purse to Janet?

8

At ten o'clock on Friday morning, Jon and I joined the line in front of the Murchison House on Third Street, the Designer Showcase House. The morning was breezy and a bit cool, but according to WILM-TV, by afternoon the temperatures would rise into the seventies. I had on a navy sweater set with navy slacks so when the day did warm up, all I'd have to do was remove my cardigan.

The Murchison House had been built by James Walker in 1876. It had served as the residence for members of the Murchison family until the Second World War when it was divided into apartments. Later the Episcopal Diocese of Eastern North Carolina used it as their offices. Now it was beautifully restored and once again served as the new owners' primary residence.

Fourteen local interior designers had decorated the interior of the house and Jon and I had heard that their work was outstanding so we were anxious to see what they had accomplished.

As the line inched forward, someone called my name and I turned to see Melanie approaching, a really handsome guy in tow.

Another new outfit, I thought, as I scrutinized the sage green pantsuit she wore; the lines were soft and flowing, not at all masculine. And her shoes, purse, and jewelry were shades of bronze. How does she do it? I asked myself. I couldn't put an outfit like that together if my life depended on it.

"Thanks for saving a place for us," she said loud enough for everyone to hear before she broke into the line.

Jon arched his eyebrows at me. I crossed my eyes, a talent I had perfected in childhood. The man with Melanie caught me in the act and grinned.

"This is Joey Fielding," Melanie said.

When Jon and I merely said "hey," she exclaimed, "Surely you know who Joey is."

Mentally I thanked her for a good excuse to look him over. He was well-built, had brown hair and brown eyes, a heart-stopping smile, and serious cheek bones. Lightbulbs went off. "Oh sure, you're one of the stars on *Dolphin's Cove*. Sorry I didn't recognize you right off." I stuck out my hand and he shook it.

I'd watched the show a few times, enough to know the storyline and who plays whom, but I had to admit I wasn't hooked on it as many were. Joey played a high-school dropout who hung around the campus often enough to have been the principal. His character who a kind of Gen X Fonzi with a little bit of James Dean thrown in for good measure—cool, somewhat arrogant, yet deeply sympathetic.

Jon, whom I know for a fact has never seen the show, said, "Good to meet you, Joey. I admire your work."

"We're looking at historic houses," Melanie said by way of explanation, "and thought we'd pop in here to check it out. We didn't expect such a line though."

She went on to tell Joey that I was her sister and that Jon and I restored old houses.

"Maybe you can restore mine when I find it," Joey said. "I've got my heart set on something like this." He looked up at the red brick mansion with its tall tower.

"Second Empire?" I inquired. "Is that what you like?"

"Yeah, this is way cool." Glancing at Melanie, he asked, "Is it for sale?"

She shook her head. "But never fear, we'll find one for you."

It isn't unusual for celebrities who come here to make movies, and for visitors who come for the Azalea Festival or the Candlelight Tour, to fall in love with our town, buy homes and stay. In the past, Alex Baldwin and Kim Bassinger had lived here for a while, and Andy Griffith, and now Linda Lavin. It seemed that Joey Fielding intended to be added to the list.

"I grew up in Litchfield," he told me, "so old houses like these seem the norm to me. Will you keep an ear out for me, Ashley? You're bound to hear when a house like this might be coming up for sale."

"I'll be glad to," I said. Then seeing the storm brewing in Melanie's eyes, I added, "But no one's better connected to the real estate scene than Melanie."

I turned to her. "I'm surprised to see you here. Don't you have festival duties to attend to?"

"There's the garden tour ribbon cutting, but Jillian's handling that. Besides, the festival officials are very aware that I've got a business to run."

"Same for me," Joey said. "My character's not in today's shoot."

"How is the show handling Mindy's absence?" I asked.

"They wrote her out. That's why they wrote me out too. Our characters are supposed to be off together, rekindling their love affair."

He grew serious. "What happened to her, Ashley? You were there. I've already asked Melanie about it, but she didn't see anything. I was in the tent, and I saw you standing right next to where Mindy was sitting when it happened."

"I'd turned my back," I explained. "She made a weird sound that alerted me something was wrong. She seemed to be in pain. She had some sort of seizure, then she was unconscious. The crown fell off her head, and the glass dropped out of her hand."

"Glass? What glass?" he asked intently. "Someone said a bee stung her."

Melanie was studying him like he was a foreign specimen.

"I don't know about that," I said. "If she was allergic to bees, her folks didn't know about it. They said she wasn't." I shrugged my shoulders helplessly. "I don't know what happened."

"But what's this about a glass?" Joey seized on it. "What was in the glass?"

I told him about how Mindy had objected to sweet tea, and how she had demanded sugarless tea. "Tiffany offered to get it for her."

"From where I was standing I saw Tiffany carry a glass of tea out to where you all were gathered, and I saw her hand it to Tiffany," Joey said.

"Yes, that's what happened."

Jon was getting impatient, fidgeting, and then the line surged forward and we reached the ticket sales table where we purchased our tickets.

"This is what I'd like to know, Ashley," Joey asked, pursuing the subject of Mindy's collapse. "Did you see who gave the glass to Tiffany?"

I frowned. What was he asking me? "What are you suggesting?" I asked.

"I'm not suggesting anything," he replied. "But I would like to know how much you saw."

How much? I shook my head. "No, I didn't see where Tiffany got the glass."

The front door opened. "Oh, look, we're next," I announced, happy that the inquisition was over. Joey Fielding was much too intense for my tastes.

We passed between leaded glass doors beneath a leaded glass fanlight and on into the main entry hall. The tour was self-guided so I took

Jon's hand and pulled him into the south parlor where the light was bright and the colors spring-like.

"What was that all about?" I asked him.

He guided me away from the door to a spot near a window. "I may not watch that show, but I do read *People* magazine. Mindy Chesterton and Joey Fielding were once an 'item.' Then she dropped him for Jimmy Ryder. Apparently, he didn't take it too well, and she accused him of stalking her. Well, they worked together, so there wasn't much that could be done about her accusation, even if it was true. How can you get a restraining order for someone you might have to shoot a kissing scene with?"

"Life imitating art? Or art imitating life?" I mused aloud.

"I don't know, but here they come."

Melanie and Joey followed us about the house, Joey asking my opinion on the things we saw, Melanie going into a deep sulk. In the dining room, the colors were dark and intimate, and the antique table was positioned at an angle. Joey wanted to know what I thought about that.

"It's effective," I said.

"I like the way the sofa's pulled up in front of the fireplace. I like the idea of a comfy place to sit in a dining room. I want that in my house. Me and my guests sipping after-dinner brandy in front of a fire, without leaving the room."

"It's nice," I said, and slipped away to Jon's side.

"He won't leave me alone," I complained to Jon.

He glanced over my head. "Maybe he likes you. Don't look now, but here he comes. Wait, Melanie's heading him off. I think she's had enough of being ignored by the 'star.' She's leading him back toward the kitchen."

Jon drew me toward the stairs. "Now's our chance. Up the stairs."

After we'd toured the bedrooms and bathrooms—my favorite was the "honeymoon" suite, a pale green room with opulent, green silk Victorian bedding—it was time to go.

We had to exit out of the rear of the house, to descend a steep, narrow ironwork open staircase that led to the back yard and the gift shop. Jon was in front of me and I had just reached out for the handrail when I felt a push from behind.

I screamed and fell at the same time. Jon whirled about and caught me in his arms. People stopped to stare, while others called warnings. "Watch out!" "Catch her!"

"Are you all right?" a woman asked from below.

I assessed my condition. With the number of people in front of me on the staircase, I hadn't fallen far.

"I'm okay," I called back.

I turned around to see what had happened, who had pushed me. Joey Fielding. I glared at him.

"I'm sorry, Ashley, it was an accident. I'm too clumsy for my own good. Are you all right?"

"I think so," I replied, angry but unsure how to direct my anger.

"I'm so sorry," he repeated.

"Well, be careful, man," Jon snapped, glaring up at Fielding. "You could have hurt her."

Melanie called from above, "What's all the fuss?"

"It's nothing," I said. "I'm okay."

Maybe it was my imagination, but I could have sworn I'd felt his hand on my back.

9

"I hope she'll recover," Elaine McDuff said. "Even though she's no friend of mine. Or Larry's."

Elaine arranged puff pastries on a silver tray. The small, light pastries were filled with brie, or broccoli with melted cheddar, and other delicious fillings I hadn't identified yet because I'd only sampled two, not wanting to make a glutton of myself.

We were in the remodeled kitchen of a seventy-year-old Tudor-style house in Forest Hills. Outside the garden tour had just ended and the homeowners were making the most of their striking, flowering garden to throw a little cocktail party for friends and others in the community.

Our hosts were friends of Jon's and he'd brought me along. With eleven gardens on the tour, we'd spent the afternoon dashing about town, from Front Street to Airlie Gardens, saving the two homes in Forest Hills for last. We'd admired formal gardens and exotic gardens, herb gardens and knot gardens, water gardens and a koi pond. There were azaleas and camellias, verbena, Confederate jasmine, and flowering kale. And overlaying the profusion of color, drifts of white dogwoods threaded the gardens together like a tatting of fine white lace.

Helping myself to a glass of red wine from an open bar, I listened to talk of Mindy's collapse. There seemed to be a lot of sympathy for

Janet Chesterton who was a popular figure on the garden club circuit. Talk of Mindy led to the inevitable discussion of Nem Chesterton's bid for mayor. He seemed to generate strong feelings: people either loved him or hated him.

The crowd here was middle-aged, and one woman said, "Poor, Janet. She really had her hands full with Mindy. That young lady is what my grandmother used to refer to as a 'rip.'"

The smell of food had led me to the kitchen, where I'd found Elaine. She stopped what she was doing and looked me in the eye. "Have the doctors figured out what's wrong with Mindy?"

"Not yet, Elaine. Mindy's still in a coma. My, these are good. Wish I could cook."

Elaine gave her head a little shake, and her soft brown waves bounced. She was a nice looking woman, comfortably round, as if she were made for motherhood—but she and Larry did not have children—so her ample shape was probably the result of sampling each and every delicacy before serving them to her clients' guests. It was the direction I'd been headed in, so I could sympathize.

"Anyone can cook, Ashley," she said, as if what she did was insignificant, "but few people can perform miracles with old houses the way you do. So they don't know what caused her coma? Is that what you're telling me?"

"I was at the hospital yesterday and all Nem and Janet could say was that they were running tests."

"Well, I hope they find out soon. I hate to see anyone suffer. Although if I were a vengeful person, I'd be sticking pins in a Mindy doll. She sure did a number on Larry."

Elaine opened the refrigerator and removed a tray of deviled eggs. "I've got to get these things outside."

"Here, let me help you." I took the tray from her.

"Oh, Mindy has her good points," I said, mindful of the lecture I'd received from Melanie yesterday about my callousness.

Elaine, who'd been carrying the puff pastry tray toward the door, stopped and said to me forcefully, "If she did, I never saw them. She cost me a lot of business over the Christmas season which is my busy time. She accused me of trying to poison her. Turned out to be the flu but the damage was already done. With her having the starring role in *Dolphin's Cove* and being Nem Chesterton's daughter, she's got a lot of clout in this town."

"But why would she accuse you of poisoning her, Elaine? I don't get it. Is she that malicious?"

Elaine glanced toward the door as if checking to be sure no one would interrupt us. "Mindy had the silly notion that Larry had a thing for her. It was all a lot of foolishness. Larry is crazy about me and always has been. But you know how egotistical Mindy is, she thinks every man is head over heels in love with her."

"But you said she did a number on him. What did you mean by that?" I asked.

"She promised to get him a role on the show. Now, Larry really misses the business, you know. He loved being part of the *Matlock* series family. That was how we met."

She got a dreamy look on her face. "I was catering a big party for Andy Griffith. What a nice man he is, a gentleman through and through. Anyway, Larry was there, and I don't know, we took one look at each other and it was like we knew. As if the only question was when. We knew the what and the how and the why. I don't know if it happens to other couples like that, but it did to us."

"Yes," I said softly. That's how I felt about Nick when I first saw him, and I think it's how he felt about me. But the "when" question was a big one. When would the time be right for us?

Elaine took a step toward the door. "Then after the series ended, and Larry couldn't get work, he changed. The disappointment was so great. He'd been up there so high, then he felt like nothing. I have to tell you, it sure wrecked our sex life."

"I'm sorry, Elaine," I said, not knowing what else to say. I get uncomfortable when women start confiding in me about their sex lives. "Well, let's get this food outside."

But Elaine wasn't budging; a torrent of emotions had been unleashed and she had to rehash them. "He tried so hard to get work. At the same time my business was growing and I needed to hire an assistant. It just seemed logical for us to keep my business in the family, so Larry joined me in the catering business. But whenever we catered a party for television people, like out there at Tiffany's yesterday, it was so hard for him to be making drinks for people who had the roles he coveted.

"Then along comes flirty, saucy Mindy, with her hints that she had Cameron Jordan's ear and she would put in a good word for Larry. So naturally he had to be nice to her. But if she thought Larry had any romantic feelings for her, she was delusional. And nothing ever came of her promises."

The door to the garden opened, and Larry strode in with an empty tray. "They're slurping up your daiquiris like they're mother's milk," he said as he refilled the tray.

"Come on, girl, get a move on," he added, and gave her tush a playful pat.

"Hey, Ashley, how's it going?" he called over his shoulder as he hurried out the door.

Warning bells were ringing in my ears. "How does Larry feel about her now that she's reneged on her promise," I asked casually, my eyes not meeting hers.

She pulled open the door. "Why, he hates her guts, of course."

10

Early on Saturday morning I took a folding chair and walked to the intersection of Market and Third. When the parade began at nine, I was ready, thermos with hot coffee in one hand, straw hat in the other.

There were marching bands and mounted police, firefighters and silly clowns, the sheriff's color guard, and street entertainers. Something for everyone. And then I saw what I'd been waiting for, Melanie, the grand marshal in an open car, waving, smiling. When she spotted me, she blew me a kiss.

I stayed until mother nature called and then, dutifully, I folded up my chair and headed home.

My house is on Nun Street, in the heart of the historic district, and I love it. It's an 1860 Victorian house with a cupola, and strong Italianate influences. The wood siding is gray, and there are Roman arches above the doors and windows that are painted white with dark red trim. White pilasters support the projecting roofs of the front and side piazzas.

The Victorian period, 1837 to 1901, encompasses a variety of architectural styles. There's Greek Revival, popularly known as the architecture of white pillars. Italianate, recognizable by it's square towers. Plus Queen Anne, Gothic Revival, Japanesque, and an obscure Southwestern style called Victorian Adobe.

My favorite room is the library, done all in ruby red. I painted the plaster walls myself, then a talented artist friend stenciled Dutch metal-leaf *fleur-de-lis* patterns on the red paint to suggest tooled leather. The draperies are heavy velvet, tied back on either side of lace curtains. My easterly facing windows emit a fair amount of sunlight in the morning and I have my coffee there. A jewel-toned Persian rug covers the heart pine floor, and is overlaid with small scatter rugs in complimentary patterns.

By today's standards the room seems formal, yet served as the family room for the first occupants of the house, a Quaker minister and his large family. The plaque outside my front door reads, "Reverend Israel Barton House." Reverend Barton lived here from 1860 until 1893 with his wife Hannah and their nine children. With three upstairs bedrooms and one bath, it must have been a tight squeeze.

On Saturday afternoon, a docent stood near the library's cherrywood mantelpiece, recounting to a group of captivated tourists how Reverend Barton had been a prominent abolitionist, and how this house had been a stop on the Underground Railroad.

The Historic Wilmington Foundation sponsors a Home Tour during the Azalea Festival, on Saturday and Sunday, with eight homes chosen for their varying architectural styles. It's a real walking tour, with most of the homes located in the historic district, not far from mine.

I was lingering, watching the tourists come and go, listening to their comments about my house and its decor when suddenly a familiar head appeared above the others and my heart thumped as joyously as a puppy dog's tail.

"Nick!" I cried and moved through the crowd to meet him, the lurching of my heart giving way to a quickened pulse, plus sweaty palms.

"Hi, Ashley," he said lightly, as if we'd parted three hours ago instead of the three months and three days since he'd left for Atlanta.

He'd promised weekend visits but had not kept his promise.

"We need to talk," he said.

"Indeed we do."

"No, Ashley, this is business."

Then I saw that he was not alone. A woman accompanied him and my heart gave another tremendous lurch before dropping into my stomach from the sheer weight of disappointment. So this is what heartache feels like, I told myself, eager to know who she was and what place she occupied in his life.

As people milled about us, and voices grew louder, Nick asked, "Is there somewhere quiet we can talk?"

I thought for a moment. There was no quiet nor private space within my house just then. "The gazebo," I said, leading the way through the reception hall, the back hall, the kitchen, and out the back door.

A hundred newly bedded, colorful azaleas bloomed in my garden but I was blind to their pretty upturned faces. I walked to the gazebo as if I were on a death march, full of dread, pain, and anxiety. Who was she? His girlfriend? Surely, not his wife. I would have heard.

The interior of the gazebo was shaded with vines of Carolina jessamine, their small yellow trumpet flowers in full bloom. Bees droned drunkenly, and I reflected fleetingly on the bees at Moon Gate and wondered again if Mindy had been stung.

Built-in seats lined the hexagonal gazebo and we each took one, automatically spacing ourselves equidistant one from the other. Aha! I observed with relief, so she's not a love interest. But who then?

Nick looked tired. He'd lost weight as I had. His hair was a bit longer, a little fuller on the sides, more stylish, and I wondered if the plainclothes officers of Atlanta PD enjoyed relaxed dress codes. As usual, his suit was finely tailored and woven of the lightest wool, and his tie was made of silk rep, with tiny, colorful lighthouses on a tan background. If he'd smile, I'd see dimples, but he wasn't smiling.

"How've you been, Ashley?" he asked.

"Fine, Nick, fine."

"Good." He looked me over but made no further comment of a personal nature. "This is Detective Diane Sherwood, Wilmington PD."

I regarded his companion. She had a nice, open face, a sincere expression, pleasant but not overly friendly. Her hair was chestnut brown, wavy, and reached the collar of her brown-on-white striped cotton shirt. Over it she wore a light camel linen blazer with gold buttons, the blazer cut full enough to conceal a regulation weapon. She had on brown tailored slacks that fit just right, and sensible brown loafers.

She gave me an earnest smile and leaned forward to offer her hand. I took it. Her handshake was firm and dry, correct. This was a woman who did everything by the book and correctly, I knew instantly. A woman of substance, not to be trifled with. And I knew something else: I liked her.

"Nice to meet you Detective Sherwood," I said. "Now, what's this all about?" I looked at them, from one to the other.

"Ms. Wilkes, we're . . . "

"Call me Ashley," I said.

She smiled pleasantly again. "For now you're Ms. Wilkes. And I'm Detective Sherwood."

I looked from her to Nick. He nodded slightly, conveying his approval.

I wondered if she knew about Nick and me, our past, our derailed love affair.

"Ms. Wilkes, we understand you were at the Talliere home on Thursday afternoon and that you were standing near Mindy Chesterton when she collapsed."

"Yes, I was. How is she?"

"Tell us what you saw, how she appeared, what you observed," Detective Sherwood continued.

Nick studied me, and I gave him a hard look, aware that neither he nor Sherwood had answered my question.

I told them about how the five of us had been talking.

"Describe where the other guests were located," Nick instructed.

I did. Melanie seated in a lounge chair next to Jillian. Mindy in another lounge chair. Tiffany and I standing. Larry McDuff moving through the crowd with a tray, offering iced tea. Elaine McDuff in the tent. Jimmy Ryder and the rest of the cast from *Dolphin's Cove* milling about, eating from hand-held plates, or seated at little tables. The mayor and festival officials lined up at the buffet tables in the tent. The belles, the princesses, the cadets. I even told them about Jon and the city councilman.

"Mindy was being rude to Tiffany, excluding her from the conversation, so I turned to Tiffany to discuss the house with her. My associate Jon Campbell and I are restoring Tiffany's house," I explained to Detective Sherwood.

She nodded. She knew. I suspected she and Nick knew everything I was telling them.

"So I had my back to Mindy when I heard her make a strange noise."

"What sort of noise?" Nick asked intently, leaning forward, elbows on knees, hands clasped.

"A kind of gurgling, and a gasping. Like she was in pain. I turned around, and she was having spasms. Her body was jerking and she was clutching her stomach. The glass and her crown were rolling in the grass."

"Tell me about the glass. Who gave it to her? What was in it? Do you know?"

"Mindy objected to the sugar in her tea. So Tiffany had Elaine prepare a fresh glass of unsweetened tea for Mindy. Then Tiffany brought it to her. Okay, my turn. What's this all about? What's going on?"

Nick and Detective Sherwood exchanged looks. "Mindy Chesterton died last night," Nick said. "We're keeping it off the front page for as long as we can."

"Oh, dear. Poor Nem and Janet. Wow, this is a shock. I was sure she'd been stung by a bee and was going to recover."

"She'd been in a coma since Thursday. She never woke up."

"Wow," I repeated. Then I remembered the festival schedule. "You said no one knows. Do the officials know? Are they going to cancel the rest of the festival?"

"We're trying to keep this out of the media for as long as possible," Nick repeated, "but we had to tell the festival officials. They're agonizing over what to do. You can imagine the position they're in."

"If they cancel, they'll disappoint a lot of people. If they don't cancel, they'll be accused of disrespect for Mindy Chesterton," Diane Sherwood said. "There's going to be fallout, no matter what they decide."

"Well, the parade was this morning, so that's over. There's only tonight's festivities and tomorrow's. I'd say they should see it through. But it might not be wise to keep her death a secret. That *would* seem disrespectful."

"It'll be front page news soon," Nick said. "She's a star; it can't be avoided. Her husband is raising holy hell, very opposed to the autopsy. There'll be one anyway. It's standard procedure with the sudden death of an otherwise healthy individual."

"Her husband? I didn't know she had a husband."

"Jimmy Ryder. Jimmy Ryder is . . . was her husband. They were married at Christmas but keeping it a secret because of the show. The rest of the cast do not know, only the producer."

"Jimmy Ryder?" I shook my head. "Jimmy Ryder and Mindy

Chesterton in a secret marriage?"

It seemed to me our small town was bursting with secrets. "Why is he opposed to an autopsy? Doesn't he want to know what killed her?"

Nick shrugged his shoulders. "He objects to having her body mutilated, was how it put it."

In a way, I could sympathize with him. His new wife, his beautiful bride, being cut up that way. "What about Mindy's parents? What do they say?"

"Nem Chesterton's badgering everyone to get it done. He's demanding answers. Mrs. Chesterton's been sedated. She's taking this pretty hard."

Of course, she is, I thought.

11

Saturday evening found Jon and me dancing at "Shaggin' on the Cape" at the Hilton Riverside pool area. The riverfront was in a party mood. Beach music filled the twilight. Out on the river, lights from flower-bedecked barges and sailboats, and all manner of small craft twinkled in the dusk. Earlier there'd been a shag contest but now the dance floor was open to all.

Jon didn't yet know that Mindy was dead. I'd been sworn to secrecy, and although it went against my natural inclination, I hadn't breathed a word. Jon, however, had not forgotten about Mindy Chesterton's medical emergency. "What do you think happened to her?" he asked, projecting his voice over the music.

"Bee sting," I said loudly. Nick and Sherry had cautioned me not to discuss our conversation.

At that moment someone tapped Jon on the shoulder, and he moved aside so quickly it was as if he had been expecting the interruption. Nick! I looked from Jon to Nick as he stepped in close and slipped his arm around my waist.

"You guys set me up!"

"Do you mind?" Nick asked.

I looked into his warm hazel eyes and knew I was a goner. "No," I murmured.

Jon gave us a wink and walked off.

Nick's smile was wide and adoring and showed off his cute dimples. "When I saw you this afternoon, all I could think about was this. Holding you. Being near you."

I melted. "You're not off the hook yet," I warned, but I pulled him closer.

This was the first time we'd danced together, and Nick didn't so much dance as he kind of swayed while embracing me. Oh, shoot, I thought. What am I going to do with this man? I can't stay mad at him. My heart and defenses turn to mush when I'm with him.

"Let's go somewhere and talk," he said in my ear.

I let him lead me off the dance floor. As we strolled away, I caught sight of Jon, dancing with Tiffany. Jon has a bad habit of picking women too young for him and then getting his heart broken. Oh, who was I to preach? Just see the trap I'd stepped into—joyfully.

We left the music behind, starting up the hill toward my house. Nick slipped his arm around my shoulders and I wrapped mine around his waist, and it was like the past three months and three days had never been and we were back where we left off.

"I must have a big sign on my forehead that says 'Doormat. Wipe feet here.'"

Nick reared back and barked out a laugh. "You! A doormat? Ashley, you're the feistiest woman I know. You're always on guard, always ready to fight. You're as scrappy as a bulldog."

I pulled away. "Nick, I haven't heard a word from you in three months, and then you show up, dance with me, and immediately we're all lovey-dovey. So, yes, I'm acting like a darned fool doormat."

"I know I owe you an apology. I was just about to make it." His expression grew serious. "I'm sorry, Ashley. Believe it or not, I thought about you every day. You were never far from my thoughts. But the case I was assigned to . . . " He shook his head. "Well, I've never had to deal with anything so difficult, and I pray I never have to again."

I believed him. And I accepted his explanation. We stopped for traffic on Front Street. "Do you want to tell me about it?"

He shook his head. "Too hard. I can't speak about the details. In general terms, I was assigned to an unsolved case involving a serial killer who'd abducted and murdered children."

"Oh, no," I murmured, "how awful for you." Under his tough cop exterior, Nick is a sensitive and compassionate individual.

He thrust his palms up and outward as if to ward off evil. "I never want to get a kid case again. We worked eighteen-hour days, seven days a week, trying to catch that monster. When I did have a few hours off, I spent them with the department shrink, it was that bad."

"I'm sorry, Nick." I took his hand as we strolled under trees, past pretty townhouses on Ann Street.

"I was in such a state I couldn't talk to anyone except the other guys and the shrink. I couldn't bring myself to call you, Ashley, much as I wanted to. I wasn't myself, and I thought I'd scare you off."

"I wish you had called," I said, wondering what kind of relationship we could ever have if he wasn't able to talk to me when he was "on the job."

He stopped for a second. "Ashley, I like to keep what's normal in my life separate from the filth I have to wallow in on some of these cases."

Once I had asked Nick if he would consider giving up law enforcement. He told me he couldn't do that any more than I could give up restoring old houses. I wanted to ask him again if he'd think about switching careers, but now was not the time. Instead, I asked, "Did you catch him?"

"Better than that," he said hotly, "I shot him. When we cornered him, he started shooting. We nailed him. Mine was one of the bullets that brought him down."

Our eyes locked. "Can you handle that? That I can kill someone and not feel remorse?"

"A child killer? You bet, I can handle it. I'd have cheered you on."

He grinned, and the mood lightened. "You'd make a cute cheerleader," he said, steering the conversation away from a morbid topic. "Thanks for understanding, baby."

We started up my porch steps. Unable to wait until we got inside, he pulled me to him and kissed me hard. "Oh, I've missed you, Ashley. Any chance you might move to Atlanta? They've got lots of old houses there for you to restore."

"What is this, Nick, a proposal?" I asked. Laughter burbled up in my throat and my spirits soared.

"Let's talk about that upstairs."

I unlocked the door and let us in. The home tour had ended hours ago, and we were greeted by peace and quiet and the fragrance of fresh flower arrangements. I led the way up the stairs.

In my bedroom, I turned on the ceiling fan. Its singsong whisper was a lyrical accompaniment to our love talk. I started to light candles but Nick wrapped his arms around my waist and nuzzled my neck. He turned me around to face him and we kissed, softly at first, then urgently until I was breathless.

My fingers found the buttons on his shirt and undid them. I lifted my arms, inviting him to pull off my sweater. We moved to my grandparents' rosewood bedstead. Helping each other out of our clothes, we slid between soft vintage sheets.

His body joined mine so familiarly it was as if we'd been making love forever and not for the first time.

When darkness was a solid black wall pressed against the windows, the first tentative explosions reverberated from the riverfront. We got out of bed to peer through the glass, catching glimpses of brilliant lights that blossomed like chrysanthemums against the sky over the river.

I pressed my face into his chest. "We're missing the fireworks."

"Come back to bed. We'll make our own."

And so we did.

12

In the morning I floated around the kitchen in a pale lavender nightgown and *peignoir*, lingerie I'd hoarded for years for just such an occasion. Earlier Nick had brought in a duffle bag from the trunk of his car. He had shaved and showered, and was wearing a clean starched shirt and a big grin on his face.

I poured coffee. How domestic we were.

My culinary skills are few, but I do know how to soft-boil eggs. That's because I collect antique egg cups and want to use them so I've taught myself not to overcook or undercook the eggs. And I'm a master at toasting English muffins.

I passed Nick butter and orange marmalade. I refrained from asking, *Isn't this cozy*? Let Nick think I dressed glamorously and breakfasted on fine china every morning. But I didn't feel awkward; in fact it felt natural to be sharing my breakfast table with him.

What a night! Wow! How many times does a girl get to experience a night like that in her lifetime? Unless you're Melanie, not often.

"What are your plans for the day?" I asked casually, feeling him out, trying not to appear possessive or needy. I had plans of my own but I'd have dropped them in a heartbeat if he said he was free.

"I've got to meet the Medical Examiner at ten." He checked his watch. "The chief asked me to lend Diane a hand."

I looked across the breakfast table and wondered why the sun shines brighter on Sunday morning? Or was it just this Sunday morning? Out in the town, church bells rang and carillons played.

Yet the bad news was out there too. The *Sunday Star-News* headlines were big and bold: DOLPHIN'S COVE STAR DEAD! I'd folded the paper and put it aside, but not before I'd skimmed the page to learn that the last day of the festival had not been cancelled.

Nick sipped his coffee, started to say something, changed his mind, then said, "I guess you're tied up with the festival."

"The house tour starts at one. They don't expect me to remain here while it's in progress. I did tell Binkie I'd meet him at the Bellamy Mansion then."

Binkie is my friend, historian Benjamin Higgins, a professor emeritus at UNC-W. Since Daddy passed, Binkie's been like a father to me, looking out for me, my protector. He had outlived all of his family, and he needed someone like me to need him.

"Then Jon and I are going to look at a garden on Front Street," I continued. "So I've got a full day planned too."

Nick looked around. "Something's missing. Where's the kitten?"

"You mean little Spunky," I said, referring to a kitten I'd rescued during the winter. "You'll never guess. Spunky turned out to be as smitten as any male where Melanie was concerned. He fell in love with her. He got so attached to her that when she left, he'd howl. I finally had to give him to her. Ungrateful beast!

So Spunky lives out on the ICW now. Melanie takes him out with her when she's working in the yard, and he has the best time stalking through the grass like a jungle creature. I'd never have been able to let him outside here in town with all the traffic."

I got up to refill his coffee mug. As I passed his chair, he caught my wrist and pulled me into his lap. "You look pretty in the morning. I didn't know I'd enjoy this," he indicated the table and the kitchen with his free hand, "so much."

I wrapped my arms around his neck and kissed his mouth. "Coffee kisses." I laughed from sheer happiness.

I nestled in his lap; I fit so well there. He pulled me close and squeezed me, then drew back. "Ashley, you're involved with an unexplained death. It might turn out to be a homicide . . ."

"Oh, Nick, do you really . . ."

"And you know that makes me crazy. You seem to be a magnet for these things . . . I want you to be very careful, especially careful. Someone might think you know more than you do about Mindy Chesterton's death, so I don't want you talking to anyone but the police. And call me, day or night, if something unusual happens."

"Unusual? What do you think might happen? You don't even know the cause of death."

"We will soon. And it doesn't feel right. Now promise me."

"I will," I vowed, crossing my heart.

I got up and refilled our coffee mugs, then took my seat across the table from him and cracked my egg shell with a spoon. I ground fresh pepper on the egg, then offered him the pepper mill.

Already I could see he was slipping into his cop's mode. If these transitions made me dizzy, how must they affect him? I was glad he had enough sense to consult the police shrink when his work got to be more than he could handle.

"My schedule's pretty tight," he said, already slipping away and toward the work before him. "As I said, the chief asked me to lend Diane a hand with the Mindy Chesterton case. With budget cuts and Homeland Security demands, Wilmington PD is stretched thin. The medical examiner is covering all the bases with this one—full toxicology screening, the works. Diane and I will attend the autopsy this morning."

"Oh, no. You've got to be there?"

"It's part of the job, Ashley. You get used to it. And I've got that other thing keeping me busy. I don't know when I'll be able to see you, but you can always reach me on my cell."

"Come when you can," I said. "Even if it's late."

I nibbled my English muffin. "By the other thing, you must mean the case you're working on with the sheriff's special task force. This is about those bodies that washed up at Fort Fisher, isn't it?"

"Yes, and we're under a lot of pressure to get that case cleared up before the beach season begins. We've got SBI agents helping, and a team of forensic pathologists from Duke. But we've got nothing to go on because we can't make identifications."

"Why not?" I asked. "Can't you make IDs from dental records?"

He shook his head. "Not with these vics. Too much damage. From the pelvic bones and cranial shapes, the M.E. verified they are males as we suspected, approximate age twenty. But that was as far as he got."

"But can't they make dental impressions then match the impressions with data bases? Aren't there some missing men you can compare dental records with?"

Nick set down his coffee mug. "Ashley, what I'm about to tell you can't be shared with anyone. Not Melanie. Not Jon. No one. Oh, I know, there'll be leaks and sooner or later it'll come out, but I won't be the source."

He looked so careworn, so weighed down with responsibility, I wanted to help. I understood he was about to tell me something important and something that could hurt him if it got out. If our relationship was to deepen and succeed, he'd have to be able to trust me, and I'd have to learn to keep my mouth shut.

"You can count on me, Nick. I won't tell a soul."

He nodded slowly, taking me at my word. "You are aware that when bodies have been in the river for a while, there's soft tissue damage. There's a certain amount of breakdown caused by the water and from striking sandbars. And the fish do damage. You know all that?"

"Yes," I said, pushing my plate away.

"Well, these cases are different. The bodies were mutilated."

"Mutilated?"

"The jaws were crushed so we can't take dental impressions."

"Crushed?"

"That's not all. The hands are missing. Some of the feet too."

"But how? Crushed jaws and missing hands and feet. Sounds like someone didn't want them to be identified."

"That's what I'm thinking."

"What about DNA?" I asked.

"The M.E. will preserve tissue samples for possible DNA identification, of course, but we've got to have someone to match it to. And for now we've got nothing."

He seemed to slip away, deep in thought, carried back to that ugly world he occupied, groping for answers. The world where evil reared its ugly head, and often prevailed. The world he was struggling to make right.

It hit me then that I respected who he was, and what he was trying to do. I'd never ask him to give up police work again. Somehow we'd build a love relationship strong enough to survive his profession.

He got up and reached for his jacket. "I've got to go. Walk me out."

At my front door, we snuggled, unable to part.

"Ashley, last night was wonderful. I want you to know . . ." He paused, pulled back and looked me squarely in the eyes.

"What, Nick?"

"I want you to know I don't sleep around . . ."

"I knew that about you," I said.

"Let me finish. Now that we're together, I won't be seeing anyone else . . . dating anyone else, that is. And . . . " He cleared his throat. "I'd like it if you didn't date anyone else either."

I took my time answering, as if I was considering his request. But what was there to consider? The only men I saw were Jon and Binkie. There was no one I wanted to date. And if there was someone else, the choice would be simple.

"Yes, Nick," I murmured in my most angelic voice.

He hugged me to him again.

"'Cause I love you, sweetheart. I want you to be mine."

"I love you too, Nick." The words came easily. I'd said them to myself often enough.

I closed the door, thinking, What a man! I hugged myself. What a sweetheart! And he's all mine.

13

A little before one o'clock I met Binkie outside the Bellamy Mansion. We took a few minutes to stroll through the Victorian garden. Mrs. Bellamy had designed and maintained and loved her garden with a passion throughout her lifetime, but after her death, it went to seed and became a jungle. UNC-W got involved, coordinating the archaeology studies that revealed the original layout of the garden. In 1996, the Cape Fear Garden Club sponsored the re-creation of the garden.

I admired showy daffodils, thrift, snowdrops, spiderwort, and cheddar pinks. Later in the summer, the day lilies and crepe myrtles would bloom.

"That poor Mindy Chesterton," Binkie declared, "the paper says she's dead. And someone said you were there when she collapsed, Ashley dear. What happened to her?"

"I don't know, Binkie. One minute she was fine, the next minute she was unconscious."

Overhead, stiff breezes stirred the branches of magnificent Magnolia trees, causing the thick, papery leaves to scrape against each other.

"But surely some event preceded the collapse. Did she eat or drink anything?"

Even though I'd trust Binkie with my life, I was mindful of my promise to Nick not to discuss the case with anyone but the police. I intended to be faithful to that promise. "I honestly don't know what happened to her, Binkie. It's a mystery."

"Poor girl," Binkie repeated, shaking his head so that a lock of snow white hair fell onto his forehead.

I reached out to brush it back and gave him a peck on the cheek, all the while suspecting he knew I was holding out on him. I hated being evasive with Binkie but what else could I do? "Let's talk about pleasant things, shall we," I suggested.

"Of course," he replied thoughtfully. Nothing much gets past Binkie.

The Bellamy Mansion had been built at about the same time as my own house, but while mine was homey, the Bellamy Mansion was grand. Visiting one of Wilmington's historic houses with Binkie is a real treat because he knows so much of the folklore of the area, as well as its history.

On one side of the property stood a sturdy, two-story brick structure. "The slave quarters," he said grimly. The large building had housed female slaves and their children before emancipation.

I let my gaze travel over the mansion. "This house was designed with our hot humid climate in mind. The white paint deflects the sun, and the generous porticos offer shade and catch breezes."

The porticos, or piazzas, as they are sometimes called, wrapped around the house, their roofs supported by beautiful, immense white columns. Small balconies projected off the second floor windows, offering air and shade. Above the entablature at the front of the house, a classic pediment rose to the roofline.

I pointed up at it. "See the belvedere. Designed to ventilate the hot air from the attic space over the children's bedrooms. And that's the original tin roof."

"There's a children's theatre but the children scarcely got a chance to enjoy it," Binkie said, "before they were whisked out of town to flee the ravages of old Yellow Jack."

"Yellow fever, you mean."

"Yellow fever. Really hit this town hard. Then, during the war, the house was occupied by Union troops. It wasn't until several years later that Dr. Bellamy was able to move his family back into their home. That was when he installed this cast iron fence."

"And that's when Mrs. Bellamy planted her garden. I'm so glad the house survived, Binkie."

"I share your sentiments, Ashley. As you know, the house was constructed by slave carpenters and free artisans, both highly skilled craftsmen."

Inside, we toured the library which an arsonist had torched in 1972. Signs of damage still remained on the south wall. The heat of the fire had been so intense, the original brass gaselier, plaster work, and slate mantelpiece were destroyed. The mantelpiece had been replaced with one made of cast iron with faux painting to look like marble. The woodwork and plaster moldings had also been recast.

After the tour, we exited into Market Street.

"Will you join me in some refreshment, Ashley dear?" Binkie invited. "My treat."

"I'd love to. But with so many tourists in town, the restaurants might be crowded. But maybe we'll get lucky. This is a good time, between the lunch and dinner hours. Shall we try the Pilot House?"

We strolled down Market to the riverfront where news of a TV star's death did nothing to inhibit merrymakers. A street fair was in full swing with arts and crafts booths, fun and games for the children, jewelry designers, potters, fancy ironwork, dance troupes, jugglers, and of course food.

The Pilot House restaurant began life in 1870 as the Craig House, constructed as the residence for William Craig, a cooper, or maker of wooden barrels. In 1977, the house was moved from Wooster Street to Chandler's Wharf and converted into a restaurant. Additions were added, including the porch where Binkie and I were being escorted to the one available out-of-doors table which was out on the new deck that extended over the river. When the city was constructing the new riverwalk, they discovered the restaurant owned a piece of the site. As compensation, the city built a deck for the restaurant that adjoined the boardwalk.

"Unsweetened iced tea," I told our waiter. In the South unless one specifies otherwise, tea arrives icy and sugary. I had no intention of regaining the seven pounds I'd lost this year, not with a lover in my life.

And that caused me to remember Mindy's very vocal and ungracious rejection of sweetened iced tea.

"Is that all?" the waiter inquired, interrupting my train of thought.

"I'll have the shrimp and grits appetizer," I said quickly. The description sounded yummy: fresh shrimp and smoked kielbasa sauteed with mushrooms, scallions, and spices, served on a fried grits cake.

"This is going to serve as lunch and dinner for me," I promised Binkie—and myself.

"I'll have the same," Binkie told the waiter. "But make my tea sweet."

To me he said, "At my age, sugar will do me no harm."

"Binkie, you're as trim as a teenager." I patted his hand. "You know, your comments about the skilled slave craftsmen who built the Bellamy Mansion made me think of Caesar Talliere. How was it that he was able to read and write in both French and English? He must have been an extraordinary man."

"He was a rarity. Not to mention that during those times, it was dangerous for a slave to know how to read and write because slave literacy was illegal in North Carolina after 1830. And Talliere arrived in

Wilmington at about 1857, shortly before the war began."

"Auguste Talliere told me Caesar was abducted from his home and sold into slavery," I said.

The waiter brought our tea.

Binkie took a sip, then said, "Talliere was brought here from French Guiana. In Suriname and French Guiana, waterways serve as their highways, connecting one village to another, so even the children master the navigational skills required to travel from one place to another. The Ndjuka had a reputation as skilled river pilots, and that made them valuable to slave traders who kidnapped them and sold them in our Southeastern port cities."

"How sad," I said, "to be stolen from your home, to never see your family again. How hard it must have been for them, and for their mothers."

Binkie nodded.

"Tell me everything you know about him. Jon and I are restoring his house. Tiffany and Auguste Talliere hired us."

"Then they chose wisely, Ashley dear, for you and Jon are the best in the business." He chuckled lightly. "I wish my students had shown your curiosity. Now let me see. In the early part of the nineteenth century, the French colonized the area that is now known as French Guiana, establishing sugar and timber plantations there. They imported slaves from Africa to work the sugar crop. Talliere's mother was one of those slaves; his father was a French sugar planter. Then, at age seventeen, Caesar was abducted and brought here.

"His navigational skills were quickly put to use for his owner. Yet in plying the river as he did, he earned a degree of freedom, so it wasn't long before he engineered an escape into the swamps. You see, at that time, he had no wife or children on the mainland to ensure his return."

"Hostages, you mean?"

"Yes, hostages," Binkie replied grimly.

"Did many slave watermen escape?" I asked.

"Yes, it was quite common. Coastal geography was in their favor. The swamps were remote, the forests dense, and there were vast pocosins where a man would drown if he didn't know where to place his feet. But that also meant there were many inaccessible places for a man to hide; places for a man to take long-term refuge. In fact, there were colonies of escaped slaves out in the blackwater swamps. That was long before the wetlands were drained."

The waiter brought our plates. At tables around us, diners basked in the sun or enjoyed the shade of an umbrella. The warm spring day offered a hint of the summer heat to come.

"In addition," Binkie continued, "fugitive slaves often found work in the naval stores industry. The longleaf pine forest generated turpentine, tar, pitch, and rosin, and there was a severe labor shortage in those remote places. So when willing laborers showed up, crew bosses asked few questions, grateful for another pair of hands.

"For a slave determined to run away, there was a network of assistance. Food would be set out, and weapons, such as a mowing scythe, the crooked handle replaced with a straight stick for use to fight the bloodhounds that pursued them. If a man or woman, or even a child, could make it to the swamps, they'd find a welcome there, a community in which to live."

I listened intently, fascinated. Binkie had a way of making history come alive; he was a wonderful teacher.

"When the war ended and the slaves were emancipated, Caesar moved back to town to a freedpeople's camp. African-Americans were the majority in Wilmington at that time, you know. And, as many were skilled artisans and maritime laborers, it was a time of opportunity for them."

"And that didn't sit well with some of the whites," I said.

"So true, Ashley. It did not sit well with some of the old guard. In fact, a violent backlash occurred. But Talliere succeeded despite that resistance. With his skill at shipbuilding, he founded his own shipyard. He built schooners for fishing and for transporting freight. And sloops and scows. He was branching out into steamers, which quickly became common after the war.

"He joined St. Paul's Episcopal Church and the Masons. He married, and built Moon Gate, at a cost of $60,000, a lot of money in those days, utilizing the same skilled craftsmen who had built the Bellamy Mansion."

"I knew he was well-to-do because of the gold coin in the bannister." I told Binkie about the coin and its significance.

"His shipbuilding business was quite prosperous," Binkie said.

"Then what happened? How did the Tallieres lose everything? Until Tiffany made money with her acting, and Auguste with his investments, Caesar's descendants had been poor. It's amazing they were able to hang on to their house and land."

"As you can imagine, Ashley dear, there was a great deal of resentment among the white citizenry for an 'uppity negro.' Yes, Caesar made a lot of money, but he made powerful enemies, as well. Conservative whites were determined to reassert the power they'd enjoyed prior to the war.

"A violent fringe organized into night riders and they tried, unsuccessfully, to terrorize freedpeoples with threats of beatings and hangings. The blacks stood up to them. Still there were isolated incidents when targeted African-Americans disappeared in the dead of night."

"Are you saying that Caesar Talliere disappeared? I'd assumed he died a natural death?"

"Vanished without a trace. Probably lynched, although his remains were never found."

14

I glanced at my watch. "I've got to go, Binkie. I promised Jon I'd meet him at the garden we didn't get to see yesterday. Would you like to join us?"

He covered a yawn with his hand. "Thank you, dear girl, but it's nap time for me. We old people need a little rest in the afternoon."

I swatted his arm. "Oh, you, you're not old, and you'll never be old. You're young at heart."

"And you look like the picture of youth yourself," he said. "You've got a glow about you." He studied me intently. "If I didn't know better, I'd say . . . oh, wait a minute, I've got it. Nick is back, someone said."

He grinned and his eyes danced merrily. "You're in love, aren't you? I can see it. It's written all over you. There's a softness about you."

I'd been bursting to share my good news. "Yes," I confessed. "It's finally happened, Binkie, I'm in love. And I'm happy."

He clasped my hands in both of his. His hands were worn and familiar, a comfort. "You're the daughter I never had, Ashley dear. If you're happy, then I'm happy. But Nick Yost should know—and indeed I intend to tell him so myself—if he causes you one moment of heartache, he'll have me to answer to."

"We've got a lot to overcome, Binkie, but this time I think we're going to make it. We're both trying."

Binkie stood, still holding my hand, and I got up too. "Seize your happiness while you are able. There's no time to waste. Nine-eleven taught us that."

As I walked my wise old friend to his comfortable bungalow on Front Street, I wondered if he had ever been in love. Someday, I'd work up the courage to ask him.

Jon was waiting for me at a house not far from Binkie's. "Hi, gorgeous," he said, his customary greeting for me. "You look stunning."

I tried to blink the star dust out of my eyes. Jon would guess, as Binkie had, and soon all our friends would know—Ashley's in love.

"You look pretty spiffy, yourself. Nice tie." I was hoping to deflect the conversation away from myself.

"The morning paper said Mindy died," he said in a rush. "Did Nick tell you what happened?"

"Jon, I don't know. Nick didn't say much about it. It was an early night for both of us." I aim to tell the truth as often as I can.

We strolled down stone steps to a sunken garden. The spectacular vista that spread before us looked like a Monet painting. And, as if painted by an impressionist's hand, the grassy green lawn was soft and lush. The delicate silver underleaves on a row of swamp birches flashed in the sunlight.

"This is fabulous," I said, impressed with the creativity of the landscaping.

There weren't as many people around as there had been on yesterday's garden tour. The festival was winding down, and many of the town's guests were on their way home.

Everywhere, garden sculpture and fountains added ornamentation, as if gilding the proverbial lily. In the near distance, Memorial Bridge—a fitting icon—arched over the river and hummed with traffic. And, of course, there were the azaleas.

Here, news of Mindy Chesterton's death seemed to charge the atmosphere like dropping barometric pressure before a storm. I passed small groups of people who were discussing the *Dolphin's Cove* star's unexplained death.

"Don't look now," Jon said, "but Joey Fielding has arrived."

Of course I turned to look. Why do people tell you not to look and expect you not to turn around to see with your own eyes?

There was a gasp among the tourists as the four male stars from *Dolphin's Cove* descended into the garden. Had they wandered in here by mistake?

Jimmy Ryder, whom I was extremely surprised to see knowing that he was Mindy's husband, stumbled on a step and grabbed onto Joey Fielding's jacket.

"Get off me, you lousy drunk," Joey hollered.

They were all drunk, stumbling, cursing each other.

"I'm calling the cops," I heard the homeowner say, and he hurried inside his house.

"Well, hello there, darlin'," Joey said, approaching me.

I wished I could evaporate from the spot. Jon moved nearer to me protectively.

When I didn't say anything, he went on, "You know my men, babe? This here's Albert Hecht." He shoved Hecht closer.

"And this handsome devil is Jeremy Summers. I say handsome devil because folks say he looks like me."

Fielding was clinging to Summers. They were all kind of hanging onto each other.

"And this is the grieving widower. Needs no introduction. The late, great Jimmy Ryder."

"Lay off, man," Jimmy snarled. He pushed Joey away.

Jon and I edged back.

In the distance I heard a siren.

"Jimmy Ryder who stole my lady. And now she's dead. If she'd stayed with me, she'd be alive today, you shithead!"

With that, Joey lunged at Jimmy and wrestled him to the ground. Jimmy staggered to his feet while Albert lifted Joey to his.

Then Joey took a swing and caught Jimmy squarely in the jaw.

Around us people were screaming.

Then for some reason, perhaps it was simply a matter of testosterone overload, Jeremy slugged Albert.

The free-for-all lasted until two cops hurried into the garden and broke it up. They called for backup and the four pugilists were driven away in police cars, presumably to headquarters.

As the police cars disappeared, the chatter-level rose like the cacophony of birdsong.

I turned to Jon. "What was that all about?"

"Looks like Joey Fielding is blaming Jimmy Ryder for Mindy's death!"

15

On Monday morning I was out on my porch, watering ferns and waiting for Jon to pick me up, when a blue and white Wilmington PD cruiser pulled up in front of my house. I wasn't expecting Nick but my heart started its little tap dance at the prospect of seeing him, so I was surprised—and maybe a little disappointed—when Melanie got out of the back seat.

She started across the sidewalk, waving and thanking the police officer who was pulling away from the curb, then hurried up the steps to me. Her eyes were wide with excitement and she began blurting out words faster than I could understand them.

"Slow down," I said, setting the watering can on the porch, and steering her inside. "Come on in and tell me what happened."

"My car!" she screeched. "My beautiful car. Someone stole it!"

I thought of the bright red Jaguar and how much she loved it.

"How did it happen? Are you okay? Wait a minute, you weren't there, were you?"

"It was a car-jacking," she cried, and raked shaky fingers through her auburn waves. "My Jag was jacked!"

"There's some coffee left. You should sit down. Come on back to the kitchen and tell me everything."

Seated at the kitchen table, with hot coffee for fortification, she told me, "I had some movies to drop off at Blockbuster. So I pulled up right in front, stepped out of the car and dropped them in the slot. It was only a few steps, but when I turned around, a punk was jumping into my front seat. I ran after him, screaming for help."

Her eyes filled with tears. Her hands shook and I stilled them with my own.

"I got ahold of his shirt, but he was too quick for me. And just a kid. He gave me a push, and I landed on my tush. Then he drove off in my beautiful car. And he's got my purse too."

"Oh, Melanie, sweetie, I'm so sorry." I slipped my arms around her. "You could have been really hurt."

"The clerk at Blockbuster called the police. They came right away, filed a report, and are now looking for my car. How many red Jags can there be in Wilmington? If he takes it out on College Road, it'll stand out like a pig in a parlor. So the police speculate he won't drive it far, but will hide it somewhere. Or take it to a chop shop."

She dropped her head in her hands, her shoulders shaking. "Oh, I can't bear to think of it, my beautiful car stripped down for parts. And I've got to get a locksmith out to my house, and at the office, and I'm too upset to think. And I don't even have a car to drive out there," she wailed.

"Well, that's easy to fix. You can use mine. Jon's going to pick me up soon, so I don't need it. And before we leave, we'll call a locksmith for you and you can meet him at your house."

"That nice young officer who drove me here radioed for someone to go out to my house to keep an eye on things, and make sure I don't get robbed."

"That was nice ... "

The phone rang.

A man's voice, throaty and rough, asked, "Is this Miss Ashley Wilkes or Miss Melanie Wilkes?"

"This is Ashley," I replied, "who do you want?"

"I'd like to speak to Miss Melanie Wilkes," he said curtly.

I arched my eyebrows and handed the phone to Melanie. "For you." Who knew she was here? The police?

Melanie said hello and had him repeat his name, then listened for a while as he spoke. Whatever he was saying was good news, because her troubled expression vanished, and she started to smile.

"I can't thank you enough, Mickey. And you'll have it delivered here, you say? And you know where my sister lives?"

Then, "Yes. And thank you again."

She hung up. "You won't believe this. A really nice man, Mickey Ballantine, found my car. He has my keys. My purse, too. And my wallet's not missing, that's how he found my name. There's not a scratch on it, he said. He's having an associate deliver it to me here."

"Mickey Ballantine? Where have I heard that name?" I asked. "And how did he *find* your car."

"I'm not sure. What difference does it make? He found it, that's all that matters. I'm getting it back. And he said the little punk who made the mistake of stealing Miss Melanie Wilkes' car is going to pay."

"But who is he? Do you know him?"

"Well, no I don't know him, but I've heard of him. He moved here from New Jersey and just opened that new club down at the riverfront."

16

"I couldn't believe it either, but they're shooting out on Harbour Island." Gus shrugged broad shoulders. "Not even the death of the star is sufficient reason to delay the production schedule. Tiffany said Mindy wasn't scheduled to be in today's shoot anyway. I know the show must go on, and all that, but this seems callous to me. The poor girl is dead!"

"I'm surprised too. I expected Tiffany to be here, but we'll carry on without her."

I carried notebooks and a camera and Jon toted his fancy new camera.

"What do I smell?" I asked.

Gus had met us at the front door to Moon Gate, and we stood talking in the reception hall. As before, the back door stood open and I had glimpses of the cypress gardens.

"Oh that," Gus replied. "I'm just stripping off the old paint in the parlor. Getting a head start and lending a helping hand."

"Are you using a paint-removal heat plate? Is that what I smell?"

"Yes, makes the job go faster and easier," Gus replied. "Come on, I'll show you." He led the way into the rear parlor.

"Yes," Jon said, struggling to maintain his composure, "you have made progress. But you have to be careful with those things. They can get overheated, especially with old wiring like you've got in the main house."

When Tiffany and Gus had converted a wing to a temporary living quarters, they'd had additional wiring installed to provide for modern appliances, a television set, a computer. But here in the main house, the electricity dated back to the days before circuit breakers.

"I'm careful," Gus assured us. "This paint is so old and tough, after the heat plate softens it, I can scrape it off easily."

"Well, you know, we're going to bring in a painting contractor," Jon said, trying to be tactful.

"Sure, I know. But I enjoy working with my hands. And this gives me something to do."

As Jon and I mounted the stairs to the second story, he complained, "The guy's an idiot, bringing that heat plate in here. Doesn't he know how risky that is? I think I'd better put the fear of God in him."

"Be careful what you say. He is the client. This is his house."

"Yes, Ashley, but I don't want to see the clown burn down his house. Anyway, it belongs to Tiffany too. Bet she's got more sense than he does."

"You like her, don't you?" I asked. "I saw you dancing with her on Saturday night."

He paused at the top of the stairs. "She's a great girl."

I smiled at him. "Well, I approve."

"Well, I don't approve of that electric paint remover. You know as well as I do that many structures catch fire during restoration. It's a vulnerable time and fires are common."

"I do know. Fire's a real threat for an old house like this one. The wood's so dry and burns so quickly, and then the fire can spread rapidly through the voids. With new structures, you've got compartmentalization and that slows fire. But in a house this old, these furred-out walls and this vast open stairway act like a flue, sucks the flame straight up."

"The brick and stone won't burn," Jon said, "but if he starts a fire, we could lose the wood framing, the sheathing, and the flooring. At least Willie knows better than to let any of his crew smoke on the job: cigarettes are a real danger too. And he always supplies a portable generator so we don't have to rely on out-dated and possibly faulty wiring to run our equipment. So will you have a talk with Gus or shall I?"

"Maybe I'd better," I said.

We moved into a large bedroom and Jon started taking pictures with his new 35mm camera. The camera was specially adapted for use with a photogrammetry computer program which analyzed pictures and calculated measurements.

"Seems to be the master bedroom," he commented. "There's a bathroom adjoining it."

"This was originally Caesar's room," Gus said from the doorway. How long he'd been standing there? "He described it in his journal. It used to be a beautiful room, and after you've worked your magic on it, I plan to make it my room."

"The proportions are graceful," I said. "It will be beautiful again."

Window panes were cracked or missing, and the wallpaper was peeling off the walls in long narrow ribbons. Signs of water and small critter damage were evident. But the decorative plasterwork and moldings were classically Greek Revival in style, featuring intertwined grape leaves and vines. The few pieces of remaining furniture were American period pieces and quite valuable.

Over the doorway that connected the bedroom to the bathroom, a transom of art glass depicted mythological scenes. Even under decades of accumulated dust, I could see that the colors were vibrant and would shine like jewels when cleaned.

Jon stepped into the white tile bathroom. "Looks like this was added in the Twenties," he said.

"It was. The family came into a little money in the Twenties. Some of my great-uncles were entrepreneurs and they spent money on updating the house. That's when the electricity and plumbing were added."

Entrepreneurs? I wondered. Or bootleggers?

"This was probably a dressing room," Jon speculated.

"I believe it was a birthing room," I said. "It was customary in better houses to use smaller bedrooms off the master bedroom for the birthing of babies. I feel sure that this was one."

Gus grinned. "You're right, Ashley. Caesar writes about the birth of his first child, my great-grandfather, the first Auguste."

Jon pointed to a small door set low in the wall. "They ran the plumbing outside the house, and built this utility chase to enclose it. Much easier than going through the plaster walls."

He opened the door and peered inside. "It's a utility chase all right. They even had the foresight to install rungs so that if repairs had to be made a plumber could climb up or down to the broken pipe."

"There's only one other bathroom in the main section of the house," Gus said, "and it's directly under this one so the chase runs outside it too."

"It was the practical way to do things in those days," Jon said. "We have better ways today."

Jon began taking pictures so Gus and I moved to the staircase. While I followed him down the steps, I rehearsed what I'd say to him about being very careful when using the paint-removing heat plate. But when we reached the first floor, I saw that the appliance had been unplugged and set safely on the fire-resistant marble hearth.

17

I met Melanie at the Rialto Ristorante. She'd called, wanting me to celebrate with her, so thrilled to have her car back. Cameron was in emergency meetings with the show's writers.

"I'm meeting Nick for dinner," I told her, "but I'll have a drink with you."

"Sure. Sit down and share this chianti with me while I check the menu."

The Rialto is a fine Italian restaurant, located on the causeway that connects Wrightsville Beach to the mainland. Owner/chef Mark Lawson won a place for himself in the community when he invited the residents of a homeless shelter to the restaurant for a traditional Thanksgiving dinner which he personally prepared for them.

The dining room was plush and romantic, with Frank crooning a song about when he was twenty-one, soft lights, and waiters who spoke in hushed tones. Murals of Venice's Rialto bridge tinted the walls in a wash of colorful pastels and the table linens were heavy.

Melanie was herself again, looking gorgeous in a cinnamon color linen suit and lots of gold jewelry. I didn't look too shabby myself, dressed up for a date with my sweetheart in a periwinkle sweater set and matching linen skirt. And slides with little heels. I'd even painted my toenails.

She looked me over. "You look nice. You should dress up more often. Nick, huh? So you two are back together." She shook her head. "You guys are like magnets. I don't know whether to worry about you or envy you."

"Just be happy for me."

She raised her eyebrows. "Oh? Do I detect a serious relationship here?"

Fortunately at that moment the waiter brought a platter of Crostini to the table so I was able to avoid answering. My relationship with Nick was too new. Part of me wanted to shout about it, while another part wanted to keep it secret.

Despite my best intentions, I ate my share of the appetizer. At my elbow, the waiter silently filled my glass from the chianti carafe.

After ordering *Pollo Marsala*, Melanie began to tell me how delighted she was to have her car and purse back, to not have to change the locks or report her credit cards stolen.

Then the waiter appeared again with a bottle of champagne which he ceremoniously uncorked. "Compliments of the gentleman at the corner table," he said, nodding to a man who sat in a shadowy corner. The champagne fizzed in tall crystal flutes.

"Who is he?" I whispered.

"I don't know," Melanie whispered back, but she lifted her glass and saluted him with it. In return, he lifted his wine glass and toasted her from his corner table. Melanie stared. He stared back. The heat between them was enough to scorch the table linens.

"I smell trouble," I said, looking up to see the man crossing the room to our table.

He bowed slightly to Melanie. About her age, mid-thirties, he was impeccably dressed in a dark suit with a dark shirt, not black, but an eggplant color. His hair was black, thick and wavy, straight nose, chiseled jaw, a full bottom lip and a cleft in his chin. His eyes, gazing at Melanie, were filled with longing.

Uh oh, how many times have I seen that look? How many times in my role as Melanie's little sister have I seen this bit of live theatre being played out? He was smitten, just like Cameron, just like Spunky, just like any male who found himself within her pheromonal zone.

He offered his hand. "Mickey Ballantine, at your service, Miss Wilkes."

Melanie cooed and gushed, and permitted her hand to be held for longer than a normal handshake. "Mr. Ballantine, please join us. Ashley has dinner plans elsewhere but I'd be delighted if you'd dine with me. I'm glad for a chance to thank you properly for rescuing my precious Jag."

Magically, the waiter was suddenly there, pulling out a chair for Ballantine, addressing him by name, swiftly setting a place for him. I was superfluous, forgotten, and I got up to leave. Heads together, Ballantine was telling Melanie, "I saw you riding in a convertible in the parade and I said to myself, that is one beautiful woman."

I said goodnight and left, thinking, yes, she'd thank him properly, but would she also thank him improperly? Poor Cameron.

18

Nick was waiting for me at a window table when I arrived at The Bridge Tender Restaurant. He kissed me on the cheek and held my chair for me. A waiter took our drink orders, then returned with my water and Nick's wine and rattled off the house specials. Between the chianti and champagne, I'd had enough alcohol. "Lobster Scampi," I said.

Nick ordered Herb Crusted Grouper. He gave me a loving look. "How's my girl tonight? You look pretty."

"I'm great," I said. Now that I'm here with you, I thought. "But Melanie's car was stolen this morning and a man named Mickey Ballantine found it and returned it. I just left them at the Rialto."

"Ballantine? He's bad news. Tell her to be careful."

"Oh, Melanie loves the risky ones. What did he do?"

"Nothing we can pin on him, but he's being watched. Left New Jersey because of some trouble there."

"Well, I love the house we're restoring," I said to change the subject. Enough of Melanie and her love life. I wanted to concentrate on my own. To talk about my day. To have Nick tell me about his. "Moon Gate is a restorationist's dream come true. Very little has been done to it in about a hundred years."

He wrapped his hand around mine. His hand was warm and solid, just like him. Let Melanie have the thrill of the chase, I'd take the real thing.

When he had called earlier to invite me to dinner, I'd detected an undercurrent of excitement in his voice. I suspected there was new information in the Mindy case. I was eager to find out what, but for the moment I was content just to look into his eyes, to breathe the same air.

Our food came and for a few moments silence reigned.

"How's the grouper?" I asked as I speared a succulent morsel of lobster with my fork.

"Perfect," he replied. "This is one of my favorite restaurants."

"Mine too," I said. There was a lot I didn't know about Nick. I thought of all the things I had to learn, and how much fun it was going to be to learn them.

Later, as the waiter cleared our plates and brought coffee, Nicked studied the water outside our window. "Some day I'd like to live out here. I've even thought it might be fun to live on a houseboat. What do you think? Could you stand a houseboat on the weekends?"

I grinned. "If you were on it, I could."

His cell phone chirped. "Excuse me, I've got to take this."

"Yost," he said into the phone. A few yeses, followed by "Later."

"Sorry about that." He lifted his coffee cup and regarded me thoughtfully.

"What?" I asked.

"There've been some developments. You might as well hear it from me, it'll all be on the news later."

"What happened?" I asked, leaning forward. Suddenly, I felt very sad. A life ended. An actress on her way up. Who knows what she might have accomplished in her lifetime? And I was standing right there when it happened.

I stared out at the marina where yacht lights twinkled in the darkness like a swarm of lightning bugs. Across the channel, Blue Water Restaurant was lit up like a Mississippi showboat.

Nick set his coffee cup in the saucer firmly and said, "She was poisoned. It was the tea."

"Poisoned?" I repeated breathlessly. "What kind of poison?"

"The toxic agents were grayanotoxin and arbutin glucoside. The M.E. says those agents were brewed with the tea leaves. So it was premeditated. Someone had prepared the poisonous tea in advance."

"What's that? Grayanotoxin? And the other thing you said. What are they?"

"Azalea leaves, Ashley," Nick said.

"Azaleas!" I exclaimed, horrified.

"The entire azalea plant is poisonous, with a toxicity level of six, the highest rating. Every bit of the plant is lethal. People have used it to commit suicide. It's in the rhododendron family and everybody knows rhododendrons are toxic. Farmers are warned to keep their livestock away from them."

"And someone put the leaves in Mindy's iced tea?"

"Someone mixed ground leaves and bark with tea leaves and brewed the drink."

"She did say it tasted bitter," I said thoughtfully. An image flitted across my mind's eye. "Oh, I just remembered something. The garnish in the ice tea glass, a sprig of mint. Was that an azalea sprig?"

"Yes, we've got the glass. And the sprig. Azalea, not mint."

"But how would someone know that Mindy would demand a second glass of tea?" I wondered out loud.

"How many people could have heard her complain about sugar?" Nick asked. "She may have done that before—made a scene, demanded sugarless tea—and the murderer witnessed it."

"She was grabbing her stomach, Nick, like it pained her," I said, remembering.

"The poison attacks the stomach and the cardiovascular system. That's how it works. It's a hell of an effective poison. And under other circumstances, might not ever be detected."

A hush fell over the restaurant, followed by an excited buzz. I turned to see the source of the commotion. Three men were being escorted to the table next to ours. As they passed I got a good look. I gasped, my hand flying to cover my mouth. "Ohmygosh! That's John Travolta."

Nick followed the trio with a policeman's sharp eyes. Voices in the room rose excitedly. I stared openly at Travolta as he sat down. His dark hair was cut close to his scalp, his expression was warm and relaxed. His eyes were lively. He looked around the room and nodded to people, like he was happy to be here, glad to be among us. A nice guy, everyone said. Grateful for his comeback.

"He's in town making a movie," I told Nick. "They started shooting this morning in the old courthouse. Travolta's character has an office there. Who are the other guys?"

Talk of homicide was forgotten as we got caught up in the moment. "Bodyguards," he said. "They have to bring their own security; we don't have the manpower to cover them."

I leaned in close. "I heard John flew his own plane here. He's a pilot, you know."

"So I've heard," Nick replied, suppressing a smirk.

"Are you laughing at me?"

"Laughing? Me?" His lips were a straight line but his eyes danced.

I chuckled. "Well, I have to confess, I'm as star struck as the next person. My neighbor works at the courthouse and they used her office for one of the scenes. She was acting so cool when she told me about it." I grinned at him. "So I just said to her, 'You mean you weren't excited to have John Travolta using your office?' And she broke out in a giggle and confessed, 'Very excited.'"

"Ashley . . ."

I turned my head for another glimpse of the movie star.

Our waiter trotted up to our table. "Here's your check," he said, tossing a small black folder down. His face was flushed with excitement, and he fidgeted. Probably a drama major at UNC-W. "We're all taking turns serving John." Already he was moving away. "Be back . . . later."

Nick pushed his chair away from the table a few inches and leaned back. "We can forget about him. We won't see him again."

I was having a hard time concentrating, my head turning from Nick to the next table. "What?" I murmured.

He laughed out loud. "Ashley, have I lost you?"

"What? Oh, no," I answered, dragging my gaze away from the famous star. "I'm sorry, Nick. We were talking about Mindy's poisoning. It had to be someone at the garden party." But who? I asked myself.

Detective Diane Sherwood hurried across the restaurant to our table. "I'm sorry to interrupt, Ashley. Nick, we've got to talk." She was dressed in another of her detective outfits, a dark brown pantsuit with a white shirt, sensible shoes. Small gold earrings, wrist watch with a leather strap.

"Hi, Diane. Why don't you join us," I invited.

Diane looked to Nick for permission.

"Sure, Diane, have a seat," he responded, indicating the empty chair at our table.

"Well, okay, but I've got to give you a heads up. Something's happened." She glanced at me pointedly.

"Ashley's okay," Nick said.

Diane hesitated, then said, "Actually, it's convenient you're here, Miss Wilkes. We're asking everyone . . . " Her glance strayed to the next table, moved on, darted back. “That’s John Travolta,” she exclaimed in a loud whisper.

Her mouth dropped open. “I can’t believe this. He’s one of my favorite stars.”

Jumping up, she grabbed her notebook from her jacket pocket. “Be right back.”

Nick threw up his hands, barked out a laugh, and said, “I give up.”

Diane was back in a minute, holding the notebook in both hands and staring at the autograph as if she expected it to disappear. “I just saw *Grease* on TV for the first time.”

“And how about *Saturday Night Fever*? I love that movie,” I said.

“Hey, you two!” Nick said.

“Sorry,” I giggled.

Diane suppressed a chuckle. “Back to business. Ashley, we’re asking everyone who was at the Talliere garden party to let us take fingerprints. I’ve got the mobile unit outside. We can do it now.”

“Sure,” I replied. “I don’t have any objection. But what does this mean?”

“We’ve got the glass, and there are three sets of prints, so we’re doing a bit of elementary detective work—process of elimination.”

“How’d you get the glass? The last time I saw it, it was rolling in the grass.”

“One of the EMT’s had the presence of mind to pick it up and take it with him. Just a hunch, but it turned out he was right,” Diane replied.

“But what about Jillian Oliver? She was there too and now she’s back in New York.”

“Miss Oliver is cooperating fully. She’s given a statement and her prints to NYPD and they’re faxing the data to us.” Then she turned to Nick and said, “I hate to break up your evening, but we need you. You can leave your car here and ride with us in the mobile unit.”

Nick didn't ask why. "Sure. I'm sorry, Ashley."

"No problem."

He picked up the small black folder. "Guess I'd better find the manager and settle this bill."

Outside, a bracing coolness had spread over the coast. The night was quite dark but lights from the marina danced on the water like a constellation of stars. For a second I lingered with Nick at the edge of the crowded parking lot, neither of us wanting to say goodnight. Luxury automobiles filled every parking slip, except for the big white mobile PD unit, the size of a small bus. A uniformed officer let us in.

The unit was high tech inside, a police station on wheels. Within minutes, my fingers were rolled on an ink pad, then pressed onto a ten-card.

Diane and Nick were deep in conversation nearby. Although they spoke in near whispers, their words carried in the small space. I overhead Diane say, "Nem Chesterton insists we conduct a thorough search of Mindy's house for clues immediately."

19

The next morning I got right to work carrying out my plan. I'd been up most of the night plotting it.

As soon as the sun came up, I unlocked the shed at the rear of my property where I store my parents' station wagon. I'd been unable to part with it because it held too many memories for me. Family vacations with Mama and Daddy, Melanie and me in the backseat; me with my sketch pad and colored pencils, Melanie with her mirror, combs, and makeup.

I was mildly surprised that the old Volvo started up so easily. Guess their reputation for reliability is well deserved. I parked it at the side door.

Back inside my house, I dragged all my cleaning supplies from the cupboards and piled them in the rear hallway. Then I got my broom and buckets and added those to the heap. Finally I wheeled my vacuum cleaner from the hall closet, out the door and into the *porte cochere*, then hefted it into the back of the station wagon.

Back inside my house, I heaped bottles of liquid cleanser and cans of furniture polish and rags into the buckets, carried them out to the station wagon, and set them inside right next to the windows where they'd be visible. A mop and broom were shoved in last.

I went back into my house for my purse and Mindy's pink satin purse, and for one final check of my appearance. I'd cut slits in the knees of my oldest jeans, and I was wearing my paint shirt over a white cotton tee shirt. My clothing was laundered, but not ironed. My hair was stuffed up under a ball cap.

I'm as ready as I'll ever be, I told myself, inspecting my clean, un-made-up face. I'm a regular Hazel.

I drove out to Landfall. By eight-thirty the air was bright, clear and yellow the way it is in spring, not hazy the way it gets in summer. Quickly I reached the white stucco walls that surrounded the exclusive community. I didn't think I could talk my way in and this time I didn't have Nem Chesterton calling ahead to pave the way for me as he had on Thursday. So now I was a maid, and determined to act calm and casual, bored even, when I confronted the guard in the booth and identified myself by my new name, Jennie Lopez, short for Jennifer Lopez. A nice touch, I thought.

But I needn't have bothered worrying, for when I pulled into the private driveway, the glass booth was empty. Up ahead a large moving van was parked, and the guard and driver were having some sort of altercation. The guard glanced my way, took in the older model station wagon complete with its assortment of cleaning equipment, and motioned for me to drive in, no doubt forgetting me as soon as I was out of sight.

"All right!" I cried, punching the air. "I'm part of the invisible class."

Again I wound around the curving roadways within the complex. Fleetingly, I recalled Mindy saying she wanted to buy Moon Gate and how determined Tiffany had sounded when she said it wasn't for sale. Had Mindy planned to sell her Landfall home?

Mindy's driveway hooked around a small grove of wax myrtles which offered some privacy from the street. I parked behind the dense bushes, directly in front of the closed garage door, then caught myself as I began hauling out the cleaning gear. Shaking my head at my foolishness, I thought, *It's not like I'm going to clean the house, for pity sakes.* All this sneaking around and worrying had addled my brain.

From Mindy's purse I withdrew her house keys, found the one that fit the kitchen door, slipped on latex gloves and let myself in. Standing perfectly still, I held my breath and listened for any sound that I was not alone.

I'm trespassing, I reminded myself, and here in North Carolina the Second Amendment is dearer to some homeowners than the Ten Commandments. I could get shot. What would I do if I got caught? But who was there to catch me? Jimmy Ryder didn't live here.

Okay, I told myself, in and out fast, that's the plan. Look under the desk. See if Nick and Diane found the envelope. See what's in it that is so important Mindy had to hide it in her own home.

"Hello! Anybody here?" I called, just to be on the safe side. What I'd do if someone answered, I had no idea. But of course, no one did. I was alone in the house.

My plan was to make a quick but thorough search. I passed through the kitchen into the dining room where the sponged gold walls glowed warmly in the sunlight.

Then into the foyer and down the hall to the master bedroom. Someone had hung up all the dresses. Janet? Or one of Mindy's friends, since I'd heard that Janet was overcome with grief. A quilted coverlet in pale gold and green was silky and unwrinkled.

Evidence of the police search was discernible by drawers not being quite closed and closet doors ajar. Mindy's computer was gone, and so were the papers on her desk.

I held my breath and knelt in front of the desk, dipped my head under it and looked up. The padded envelope was still there!

With my gloved fingers, I unpeeled the tape. On my knees on the carpeting, I opened the flap and slid the contents of the envelope out on my lap.

A compact disk.

Nick and Diane should have this, I thought, slipping the disk back into the padded envelope and taking it with me.

I was mindful that the police now had my prints on file. I would be sure to wear latex gloves when I mailed the envelope and its contents to Diane. But before I did, I'd insert this disk into my computer and see what was on it. Why not? I asked myself. I'm the one who found it; surely that entitled me to some privileges.

I went upstairs to continue my search for clues. Two guest rooms upstairs, each beautifully decorated, furniture expensive. Mindy's clothes filled the closets, coats and jackets, her grandmother's famous pink satin Azalea Belle ballgown.

I slipped my gloved hand into pockets, looked inside shoe boxes, searched purses, found nothing of interest.

I stretched, then checked my watch. Ten o'clock. So much for getting in and out fast.

A sound in the street alerted me. Moving over to a window I looked down into the street. A car had pulled up, a black Porsche Boxster. Heather Thorp and Brook Cole got out and started up the sidewalk.

I was crouched down at the upstairs balcony railing when they came in the front door.

"What a mess!" Heather said as she closed the door behind them. "When Janet asked me to select a dress for Mindy, I was like, Whoa! I hate the bitch. But what could I say? They've got Janet pumped so full of Valium, she's a zombie."

"Poor Janet. She's really a basket case. Guess she thought that because we were on the show with Mindy, we were her friends," Brook replied as she sashayed in behind Heather.

I flattened down behind the balustrade.

"Like, I hate to speak ill of the dead," Heather said, "but that Mindy was a piece of work. I'm like, wow! I have no regrets that she's gone."

"Yeah, awesome. But that worked to our advantage. I'm not a bit sorry for what we did. Now we'll be rid of that Tiffany Talliere, and they'll have to give us bigger roles. There's no one left. Just me and you, girlfriend." They gave each other a high-five.

Heather twirled around in a dance. "Just us. The new stars of *Dolphin's Cove.*"

"Keep it down," Brook warned. "I think the maid's here. Didn't you see that old clunker out in the driveway with all that cleaning stuff? H-E-L-L-O! Anybody here?"

Huddled on the upstairs hallway balcony, I thought, uh oh, they've seen the station wagon. What a nerve. Old clunker, my eye. The Volvo had a nice shiny coat of dark blue paint. What did they mean by not being sorry for what they'd done? Were they confessing to Mindy's murder?

"Well, she's not here," Heather said. "Probably taking a coffee break with one of the neighbor's maids. Like Mama always says, *they'll* steal you blind when you aren't looking."

"And that Tiffany, with her black blood, ought to be waiting tables instead of starring in a show with us, as if she was as good as we are," Brook said.

I peeked between the balusters down into the great room and the open foyer where the two young women stood talking. Heather, with her long black, silky hair and big brown eyes was dressed in capri pants with a cropped tee shirt.

Obviously, they hated Mindy. But did they hate her enough to kill her?

Brook, with her fine blonde hair and runway model looks, was wearing hip-hugger jeans and platform shoes with a peasant blouse.

What are they doing here? I asked myself. Getting a dress? Ohmygosh! They were selecting Mindy's burial dress. So her body had been released by the medical examiner to the mortician, and Janet had given Heather and Brook a key and asked them to select an outfit for the funeral.

One thing I did know, everyone in town would attend Mindy's funeral. Not out of regard for her, but for the sensationalism of it all. It would be like a freak show with Mindy's defenseless dead body on exhibit. People can be so cruel. Again, my heart went out to Janet and Nem. And Mindy's brothers.

Brook's snicker carried up the stairs to me. "Well, you've got every right to hate her guts, after what she did to you." She snapped her fingers. "Stole Jimmy Ryder right out from under you, quick as that."

Heather placed her foot on the step and I scuttled out of sight, diving into the first bedroom I came to.

"No, sugar," Brook called, "not up there. Her bedroom is down here."

On hands and knees, I crept back to my post at the balustrade.

"I've never been in her house before," Heather said as the two women moved toward the dining room. "Not bad. But like they were paying her way more than us."

"Not any more. That's over. Come on, let's not take all day. Bad enough we're stuck with this miserable assignment," Brook nagged.

I stayed put right where I was and didn't move a muscle. Maybe I'd hear more.

The women's voices grew distant until they were just a faint murmur drifting from Mindy's bedroom, a murmur that was frequently punctuated by loud laughter.

It wouldn't take them long to select a dress because they couldn't care less what Mindy wore when she went to her eternal rest. They'd be leaving soon and I could resume my sherlocking.

"Okay, that's done," Heather's voice rose from directly beneath the balcony. I crawled over and peeked down. "If it weren't for Janet, I'd trash this place. That whore stole my role and she stole my man!"

Brook's snort carried to the landing. "Well, you've got every right to hate her guts. I know he was in love with you. How she roped him into marriage, I'll never understand."

"Like the oldest trick in the book," Heather retorted with disdain.

"No! You don't mean it. She told him she was preggers!"

"Like, what else? When he found out she wasn't, that he'd been tricked, he went ballistic. That's when he started drinking and got into that jam with the Raleigh police after that rock concert. That's why he's been in rehab until a month ago."

"That little slut. What a dirty trick."

"And . . . she was sleeping around while Jimmy was away."

"Oh? Who?"

"I know for a fact that one was Mickey Ballantine."

"Oooh, Mickey. He's way sexy, in a rough sort of way, if you know what I mean. I wouldn't mind a hickey from Mickey."

"But he's dangerous, shug. Everyone knows he's connected."

Connected? Oh, no, Melanie!

"You said 'one.' Were there others?" Brook asked.

"Sure there were others. You know how slutty Mindy was. And you'll never believe who. He was ..."

The door slammed shut with a bang. I waited until their voices were distant murmurings and I heard car doors slam. Then I stood up and brushed myself off, regretting that I'd missed the name of Mindy's other lover.

In a large hall closet I found a file cabinet and started pawing through the files. If there was a will, it wasn't here, but maybe the police had taken it. So I didn't know who gained from her death. Surely Nem would have seen to it that Mindy had a will after she started making big bucks. Probably in his office.

There was a folder labelled "Larry McDuff," but it was empty. So there had been some connection between Mindy and Larry, just as Elaine had suggested. Had the police taken the contents of the file? Could Larry have been the other guy she was fooling around with while Jimmy was in rehab?

Back in the great room, I noticed how footprints showed distinctly on the freshly vacuumed plush carpeting: my sneakers, Brooks' platforms, Heather's heels.

So engrossed was I in trying to make sense of what I'd just learned, I almost didn't hear the scraping of a key in the front door lock. What is this, Grand Central Station? I'd never have time to search the house with all the people coming and going.

I raced into Mindy's bedroom just as the front door swung open. Jumping into a walk-in closet, I hastily thrust aside clothes on hangers and squeezed face-inward into the corner. I sucked in my belly and pressed my nose against the wall.

Although the closed door and the clothing muffled sounds, I was able to hear someone moving around in Mindy's bedroom. The footsteps were heavy so I assumed the intruder was a man. Noises like doors and drawers being pulled open sounded. He was searching the desk.

Then the closet's double doors were flung open and he began pulling boxes off the shelf, opening them, then tossing them onto the floor. He was so close I could hear him breathing. But with my face turned away I couldn't see him. I held my breath and pressed further into the corner.

Then he left, not bothering to shut the doors. I didn't move.

I heard dull thuds as drawers were banged shut, footsteps, then the sounds of searching. The man was moving from room to room, opening doors as he went. He must have gone into the kitchen because for a time I heard nothing. A moment later, the stairs creaked. I stretched and breathed. Should I try to make a run for it? Dash out of the closet and out through the sunroom to the kitchen. Just as I decided that was my best course, I heard him coming back down the stairs. Too late.

He was back in the bedroom again, standing squarely in the closet door, blocking the light. Any second now he'd start moving clothing, then I'd be discovered.

A door banged at the front of the house, followed by girlish voices. The man drew in his breath, then bolted. Distantly, I heard his footfalls on the sunroom's flagstone flooring.

The women's voices grew near, chattering brightly. Heather and Brook had returned.

"How could we forget underwear?" Brook was saying. "She'll need a bra."

Drawers were being pulled open. "Take that one, and the other things. Who cares. Grab them all. Let Janet sort them out. Let's get out of here. I'm sick of this."

"I thought I closed those doors," Heather said and gave a closet door a kick.

After a moment, the front door banged shut again. I counted to one hundred and sneaked out of the closet. Had the man left too? Was I alone? I sneaked out into the hall but heard and saw no one.

In the great room everything looked the same but the plush carpet revealed a new set of footprints. Imprinted over the smaller female shoe prints was a trail of large, man-sized footprints that led to the stairs and back again.

So I was right, the interloper had been a man. What was he looking for? And why had he searched the entire house? And how did he get Mindy's front door key?

I hastened to the window and looked out but the street was quiet. I shared Heather and Brook's sentiments exactly: I also wanted out.

20

Carrying the padded envelope with the disk and leaving the house by the front door, I dashed across the lawn to my car. Sliding behind the wheel, I pulled the ballcap off my head and ran my fingers through my hair, curly now from the sweat of fear. I tossed the padded envelope onto the passenger seat.

The guard waved as I exited Landfall, and I waved back, one worker bee to another. Traffic on Eastwood Road was heavy. At the intersection to my right, road construction blocked two lanes. Seeing a break in the traffic, I zipped across the highway, aiming my car left in the direction of the waterway. A native, I know all the alternate routes. Right before the bridge approach, I hooked a right onto Airlie Road. The traffic here was light and the road would bring me out on Oleander and I'd take it back to town.

I passed The Bridge Tender Restaurant on my left, and recalled my dinner there with Nick last night, how he teased Diane and me about the fuss we made over Travolta. On my right, large houses sat well back from the road on manicured lawns. The road curved inland. I drove under a canopy of over-arching live oaks, fighting off memories of Daddy's accident.

On Christmas eve when I was a freshman at Parsons and home for the winter break, Daddy had been killed on this stretch of road. He'd lost control of the car he was driving, not this Volvo because Mama usually drove it, but his own, and slammed into a live oak tree. He died in the ambulance. He'd swerved to avoid hitting a golden retriever that had wandered onto the roadway. How like Daddy to risk his life to save a dog. But as a result, this stretch of Airlie Road always fills me with melancholy and I generally avoid it.

Deep in thought, I failed to notice the truck behind me until it appeared as a menacing monster in my rear view mirror. Startled by the way it was bearing down on me, I accelerated. But he stayed with me, just inches away. He's going to rear-end me, I thought, almost paralyzed with fear. I leaned on the horn, trying to warn him, but it didn't do any good. What was wrong with that idiot?

My spine went rigid and my arms tensed as I gripped the steering wheel. Frantically, I looked for a place to pull off on the shoulder. There was none, just two narrow lanes of roadway, a fence on one side and dense trees that grew right up to the pavement on the other.

"I'll pull over just as soon as I find a place, you asshole!" I yelled at the driver I could not see. Then, I thought, well, at least I can slow down and force him to do the same. I tried that ploy, gradually decelerating. But the truck, a rusty clunker, did not. I felt a thump and braced myself. He was ramming the rear of my station wagon. My hands flew off the steering wheel. The car leaped forward. I grabbed the wheel, regaining some control over the car.

"Stop that!" I screamed in my rear view mirror. "Are you crazy?"

I tried to get a look at him but sunlight glinting off his windshield made him invisible. All I could see was what I thought was the shape of a head in a baseball cap.

The truck slowed, giving me a bit of distance. Thank you Lord, I muttered, then screeched, "Holy shit!" He was only creating a little distance so he could pick up speed. He came barreling into me. His bumper, higher than mine, rammed the tailgate. The Volvo shot forward, the steering wheel flew out of my hands, and the next thing I knew I had crossed the white line and was speeding toward an oncoming black Mercedes. I fought to control the car. Dead ahead on the left, the driveway to Airlie Gardens cut a ninety-degree angle into the pavement. Yanking the wheel and standing on the brakes, I skidded off the road, just missing the oncoming Mercedes.

The Mercedes' driver honked a warning, braked and came to a screeching halt. The rusty clunker pickup roared off toward the intersection.

I dropped my head on the steering wheel. My heart was galloping. Someone approached my door, tapped on the glass. I lowered my window.

"Are you all right, Miss?" a man asked anxiously. I recognized him as the man who had delivered Melanie's car to my house.

A second man got out of the backseat and approached my window.

"Miss Wilkes? Is that you?"

"Mr. Ballantine?"

"Are you injured, Miss Wilkes?" His face was a mask of concern.

"I don't think so." My neck was a little stiff. I hadn't hit my head. My seat belt was fastened. I massaged my neck. "I think I'm okay."

"That damned fool almost killed you. I saw the whole thing. That was deliberate."

"I'm okay, really, I am. Did you get his plate number?"

"Did you notice the plate, Tony?" he asked the driver.

The driver shrugged. "Happened too fast."

Someone was out to get me, that I knew. Ballantine was right, it was deliberate.

"That truck is long gone by now," I said, trying to laugh it off. The last thing I wanted was involvement with Mickey Ballantine. "Probably some teenagers out joy riding. Right now they're probably scared witless by what they did and are hightailing it home."

"We'll drive you home. Come on," he ordered.

I caught him scanning the interior, taking in the pails and mops, my attire, the vacuum cleaner. He looked from them to me, his eyes hard; he said nothing.

My temples started to throb. "I appreciate the offer, but I think I can drive. I'd just like to get home and have a good, strong cup of tea." A good strong slug of Jack Daniel's was what I had in mind. "I'm okay."

"If that's what you want," he said coolly. "We'll wait till we know your car can make it."

"Thanks," I called, putting the car in reverse and raising the window. I tossed him a wave. Backing out onto the road, I pointed the car toward home. In my rear view mirror, Mickey Ballantine wore the expression of a very puzzled man.

Later I'll laugh, I promised myself. But not now. Ballantine was right. Someone had just tried to kill me!

As I was crossing College Road, my hands gripping the wheel, one eye on the rear view mirror for the truck from hell, my cell phone played a tiny version of "Carolina Moon." I grabbed it up.

"Meet me for dinner tonight, will you, shug," Melanie said. "We've got some catching up to do."

"Mel, someone just tried to run me off the road," I cried.

She said in a rush, "Not surprising. No one knows how to drive these days."

"No, Melanie, you don't understand. This was deliberate."

"Deliberate? Oh, you're always so melodramatic. I took off a couple of hours this morning, and now the secretary's calling me with emergencies. Deals falling through, temperamental clients. That office falls apart if I'm not there. But no matter how miserable my life gets, yours always has to be worse."

"And you're insufferable, Melanie Wilkes. Do you know anyone who drives a rusted-out clunker truck?

She sniffed. "Only half the rednecks in New Hanover County."

"Well, I'm telling you, someone tried to run me off the road. I think he was tying to kill me."

"I have too many worries of my own to encourage your delusions. Nem Chesterton left a message that he wants me to sell Mindy's house—appraise it, dispose of her stuff, everything. Janet's too upset to handle anything, he said. After a decent interval, of course. Listen, shug, I've got to go. I've got calls to make. See you tonight."

21

Flashing blue lights on top of a police cruiser got my attention in a hurry as I turned into Nun Street. Something is wrong with this picture, I told myself. Under a canopy of old oaks, Victorian-era homes sat peacefully on small green lawns, colorful azaleas bloomed around foundations, lace curtains hung in windows—all seemingly tranquil. Yet someone's burglar alarm was whooping like an exotic bird's mating call, causing my neighbors to rush out of their houses to stand in the street, and bringing the police. At the Verandas Bed and Breakfast, several guests stood watching from the upper and lower porches.

The trouble was at my house, naturally. My neighbors are all model citizens and never cause problems. I pulled around the cruiser, parked in my driveway, and stared with increasing anxiety at the two uniformed police officers who stood on my porch.

"You Miss Wilkes?" one shouted to me.

Something was wrong, really wrong. I walked around to the front porch and mounted the steps. "Yes. Have I been robbed?"

"The door's closed and locked, so it doesn't look like anyone broke in," he answered loudly. "More like vandalism."

Shards of glass glittered on the glossy gray of my painted floorboards. My sidelights are original to the house, made of wavy, hand-blown glass;

one had been shattered to smithereens.

"Can you turn that thing off?" the other officer yelled.

I inserted my key in the lock, stepped inside with the officers breathing down my neck, tapped in my code and turned off the alarm. Blessed silence.

Then the phone started to ring. "That's probably the security company," I said.

"Let it ring while we take a look around. I want you to stay right out there on the porch while we secure this place."

Glass littered the floor inside too. I took a step back and stumbled, looked down to see what had tripped me.

"Don't touch it!" the officer said. "Now there's what broke your window."

The three of us stared down at a red brick, a piece of paper wrapped around it and secured with a rubber band. The first officer pulled a pair of latex gloves from his pocket, inserted a hand in each, then bent and picked up the brick. He removed the paper.

Crudely printed on a sheet of white paper were the words, "Mind your own business or the next time this brick will be aimed at your head." Crude but effective.

"I'll take these back to headquarters. Might be some prints on the paper. The brick will be useless for prints. You stay on the porch, like I told you, Miss, while we look around."

I withdrew to my wicker porch swing. My neighbors stared up at me. I swallowed a lump, then waved. Cars were slowing as they drove by, one stopped.

My head was swimming. I leaned back against the cushions and closed my eyes. The swing sank as someone joined me in it. I opened my eyes, so glad to see Nick, his handsome face all worried and full of fear. He picked up my hand and held it tightly.

"Are you all right?" His voice sounded scared.

"I'm okay. It's just a shock. I wasn't here when it happened."

"Thank God for that." He slipped his arm around my shoulder and pulled me close.

"Two officers are looking around inside, making sure there wasn't a break-in. But that's not what it was, Nick. Someone threw a brick through the window with a warning note."

I recited the message on the note. He reached out to push a strand of hair off my forehead, noticed my shabby outfit for the first time, but dismissed it quickly. "This is what I was worried about. Someone thinks you know more about the murder than you do. You don't know anything, but they don't know that."

Guilt overcame me, and I was afraid it would show on my face, so I lowered my head and covered my eyes with my hand. I tried not to think about searching Mindy's house, or about the compact disk in a padded envelope on the front seat of my car. Someone knew I had it! Someone dangerous. Mindy's killer?

I wanted to hand the envelope over to Nick but then I'd have to explain how I'd snooped in Mindy's house and he'd never trust me again. So I said nothing; let him think I was upset.

I'll never meddle again, Nick, I promised him silently.

The two officers returned to the porch, and Nick rose to shake their hands. "Find anything?"

"It's secure in there, Nick. This is what broke the window," one said, pointing with his shoe at the brick. "We'll take it in, see if there are any useful prints. Now Miss Wilkes, I'll need some information for our report."

While I answered questions, Nick put on latex gloves and picked up the brick and the note. He cast me an anxious glance, set it back down, then strode into the house to check things out himself.

After the officers left, he lingered, wanting to reassure himself that if was safe to leave me. The alarm people were on their way to fix things, and a glazier was coming to install a new window.

"I wish I could stay," he said, holding me close, kissing me. "You'll be okay. He won't be back. Too much commotion. Oh, damn . . . "

His cell phone rang. He took the call. "Who? What's the address. Jeez. I'll be there."

"Sorry, sweetheart, gotta go." He moved toward the door. "You know Larry McDuff, don't you? Poor S.O.B. just killed himself."

22

While the glazier worked on the sidelight, and the ADT technician reprogrammed the alarm, I huddled in an arm chair in my red library, watching the local news. TV crews were on the scene, out in front of Larry and Elaine McDuff's Colonial Revival house on North Fifteenth Street in Winoca Terrace. I could see the gate to Oakdale Cemetery in the background. Now that's a spooky place if ever there was one, and I wondered idly if Elaine and Larry had felt comfortable living so close to it. The cemetery is haunted, and that is a fact.

News reporters queried each other, speculated on what had happened, hinted that they knew more than they did. A woman reporter, every hair in place, wearing an outfit that was perfectly color coordinated, said next, "Lawrence McDuff, age 37, has died of carbon monoxide inhalation. Larry McDuff, nationally known as a regular on the *Matlock* series, was reported by neighbors to be in good health, and described as a cheerful man. "His body was found in his car inside his closed garage with the car motor running.

"The person who found Mr. McDuff was a fifteen-year-old boy who mowed the McDuff's lawn. When he opened the garage door to get the lawn mower, he saw exhaust fumes, heard the car engine running, and saw a figure inside the car. He ran next door for help and that neighbor called 911.

"Mrs. McDuff was not at home. Elaine McDuff runs a successful catering business called 'Catering by Elaine.' Police have summoned her.

"A woman is approaching now. Police are escorting her to the house."

The reporter was on the prowl, microphone extended. "Mrs. McDuff? Are you Elaine McDuff?"

The camera panned around, catching Elaine McDuff in the act of raising a hand to shield her face.

"Mrs. McDuff. Did you have any indication your husband was suicidal? What are you feeling right now?"

Elaine looked stricken and bolted.

The reporter had no ethics, no compassion. Once again she was smiling into the camera, her hard eyes glittering with excitement, jabbering on.

"You vulture!" I shouted, and clicked off the remote. Disgusted, I got up. "Work to do," I told myself.

I saw the glazier and the ADT technician out, then like any diligent police officer, I slipped on latex gloves before going out to the Volvo. I unlocked it, and retrieved the padded envelope. I won't even look, I told myself, as I gathered together mailing tape and a magic marker.

I had just pulled out a length of tape, not easy to do while wearing latex on your fingers, when the thought of what might be on that disk proved to be irresistible. I'll never change, I thought, I'm incorrigible.

I inserted the disk into my computer and copied it to my document file. What to name it? I searched my memory banks. "Latimer House," I said out loud. Should anyone ever look on my computer for the file, they'd never think to look under "Latimer House."

Then I put the disk back in the envelope, taped it securely, and addressed it to Detective Diane Sherwood, Wilmington P.D. I took a hot shower, letting the water run on my sore neck, then put on decent clothes. On my way to Moon Gate, I detoured to the main post office, stood in line, and sent the envelope to Diane by overnight mail, using a made-up return address.

I'd already missed half a day of work by playing detective. Never again. From now on I was going to be so good I would bore even myself.

23

"It wasn't suicide," Melanie declared.

"How do you know?" I asked.

The air was warm, caressing my skin like silk. At dusk, the river was a prowling, living thing that had absorbed the last bit of daylight and reflected it back, all shiny and shimmery. Across the Cape Fear, Eagle Island crouched low in the water, dark and secretive, a black profile of stunted trees.

Stark contrast to the festive mood on the porch of The Pilot House Restaurant with its merry lanterns and cheerful voices. People strolled along the Riverwalk. Melanie and I sat at a table near the rail, watching them, exchanging news. I told her all about someone throwing a brick through my window and the warning note.

"What did they mean? Mind your own business? What have you been doing?"

"Nothing," I replied demurely. "Nick believes the murderer thinks I know something because I was right there when Mindy drank the tea."

"Well, so was I. No one's thrown a brick through my window," she said. Melanie can be so self-righteous at times.

"Yes, but someone stole your car!"

"Ooooh, do you think that was related to the murder?"

My cup of Carolina Bisque arrived, creamy and buttery, filled with shrimp, scallops, bits of sweet crabmeat, a hint of sherry: coastal comfort food. The old Ashley would have ordered a bowl, but the new Ashley—in love, rediscovering her waistline—settled for a cup. And a small salad, dressing on the side, thank you very much.

"Who knows?" I was glad to steer the conversation away from myself and my feelings of guilt. "Now what did you mean when you said Larry's death wasn't a suicide?"

I hadn't spoken to Nick since he left my house earlier that day so I had no updates on the latest fatality. All I knew about Larry McDuff's suicide was what I was hearing from the local newscasters. On the six o'clock news, they'd dredged up old footage of the *Matlock* series, scenes with Larry as one of the regulars.

"I had cocktails with Mickey," Melanie said, twirling a strand of auburn hair around her finger. She got a look on her face and a tone in her voice that made warning bells go off in my head.

Oh, no, I thought, she's taken with him.

"Mickey has friends everywhere, high and low," she said.

Yeah, I thought, and one of his lowlife friends stole your car.

"He's one of Nem Chesterton's biggest supporters," she said.

"Why does that not surprise me?"

"Ashley, don't be churlish. Nem's not so bad. He'll be good for business."

"He's still running? With his daughter just being murdered!" I exclaimed, incredulous.

"He's broken up, of course, but he said she wouldn't want him to quit. She wasn't a quitter, and she wouldn't want him to quit either. Besides—and he didn't say this, I am—there's the sympathy vote to consider. A lot of people vote with their hearts and right now the compassion for Nem is overwhelming."

Good thing the election's not till November, I reminded myself.

Our salads came, and even though mine was supposed to be small, the serving was mighty generous. Still all that green stuff couldn't hurt me, I told myself, dipping my fork sparingly into honey-mustard dressing before piercing baby spinach. Melanie was having shrimp salad.

"So," I said, "what's all this got to do with Larry McDuff's suicide?"

Melanie leaned closer and confided. "Well, that's just it. It wasn't a suicide. It was a homicide."

She lifted her eyebrows and gave me a knowing look.

"So you say," I said, growing exasperated.

"Don't you go getting on your high horse with me, Ashley Wilkes. Why, I used to help Mama change your diapers!"

"Melanie, just spit it out. Tell me."

"Well," she drew out the word dramatically and looked around to make sure no one was listening. "Mickey has a source in the police department."

"A source? What is he? A Soprano?"

"Hush up and listen. There was a typed confession found on the seat next to Larry. It said, 'I loved her, but she didn't love me. I'm sorry I killed her,' or words to that effect. But it was typed, so anyone could have written it. Anyway, the same toxicology expert who examined Mindy's remains for poison, ran extensive tests on poor Larry. And they found drugs. He'd been drugged before he was put in that car."

She gave me a triumphant look, as if to say, There!

"Well, for pity sakes. Why in the world would anyone want to murder Larry McDuff? He was just a washed-up actor, kind of pathetic."

"I know. But the police have now got another unsolved murder on their hands. I'm afraid you won't be seeing much of your detective, shug. Of course, their first suspect was Elaine—it's usually the spouse, Mickey says—but she was surrounded by people all day and has an airtight alibi."

The waitress took our salad plates and we ordered decaf espresso.

When she was out of earshot, Melanie continued, "I've been out to see Nem and Janet, to extend our condolences. They're trying to reach their sons, Hugh and Nem, Jr. They're college seniors, you know, Mindy's big brothers, and are using spring break to check out Boulder where Hugh will be going to graduate school. Oh, and by the way, the funeral is going to be on Friday, private, just immediate family. They don't want those ghoulish reporters hanging around."

I sighed, losing patience; Melanie spoke as if attending Mindy's funeral was something I'd been looking forward to.

She went on, "Now, we've got to talk about Mama."

"Oh, Mel, I feel so guilty. I haven't been out to see her in a week. Last Tuesday was the last time, before the festival and Mindy's death."

"Well, things were a little slow in the office this morning, so I took off a few hours to drive out to see her."

Our mother was institutionalized for dementia at Magnolia Manor Nursing Home. Her doctors guessed it was Alzheimer's disease but they weren't really sure. With Alzheimer's there is no way to make an absolute diagnosis until the patient dies.

"Ashley, honey, don't look so glum. Mama's doin' great. The medication she's on has made such a difference. She keeps saying she wants to go home. Not to our old house out there on the waterway but to her childhood home back in Savannah. I had a talk with her doctor and he said if we had someone to look after her, she could live at home again."

"Aunt Ruby!" I cried.

"Two minds, brilliant as one," Melanie said with a big, goofy smile.

I love her when she smiles like that, the way she used to when we were kids. Well, actually, I love her even when she's exasperating, but it's easier to love her when we are acting in sisterly concert.

"I called Aunt Ruby, just feeling her out."

Aunt Ruby was Mama's older sister. "She's a retired nurse, Mel. She's perfect. Will she do it?"

"Well, she didn't commit herself, but she's coming up here to see Mama and to talk with the doctor herself. If this works out, it'll be perfect. Mama won't have to stay in that nursing home, she'll be able to live in the house where she grew up."

Aunt Ruby had never married, had continued to live on in the family homeplace after their parents died.

"And Savannah's not so far. We can drive down to visit her, easy," I said, recalling how I loved the charming city where I'd done graduate work in historic preservation.

Reaching across the table, I gave Melanie a high-five. "You're the best, big sis."

"You're not so bad yourself, baby sister."

After dinner, I got home fairly early. There was something I'd been meaning to do. I turned on my computer, clicked on my document file, and opened the file called "Latimer House."

The file seemed to contain pictures and it took a moment for the pictures to scroll down and open fully. The first picture was of Mindy, her head appeared. Then her shoulders. Then her bare breasts. Then her bare everything.

Ohmygosh! Nude photos of Mindy. Now the file was fully loaded, and I paged from one nude photo to another. She seemed comfortable in the pictures, flirting with whoever was behind the camera.

In one photo, the blurred image of a man appeared, his profile to the camera, about to join Mindy on the bed. All I could see was a blurry face, and dark brown or black hair. Assuming he'd set the camera to take a photo of the two of them, I tried paging down to find it, to see who he was.

But that was the end of the series of pictures. Mindy's mystery photographer—mystery lover?—remained a mystery.

24

When I drove to Moon Gate early the next morning, I found work progressing smoothly. Plumbers, electricians, and carpenters were practically tripping over each other in their haste to get things done. After I verified that everyone was doing what he was supposed to be doing, I joined Willie Hudson, our general contractor, out on the portico steps.

"How you doin', buddy?" I asked.

"Nothing wrong with me bein' forty again wouldn't cure," he replied tartly.

I laughed. "You must be okay, you're feisty."

He gave a hearty laugh. "I like that young Miz Talliere. She's here now, you know. Doesn't have to be on the set till later."

"Well, good, I need to speak to her."

"You know, I been hearing 'bout the Tallieres all my life. They go back generations; so does my family, Miz Wilkes."

Willie was from the old school and wouldn't dream of calling a white woman by her first name.

"I've been hearing a lot about them myself lately. And when are you going to start calling me Ashley?"

"When you are you going to start calling me Mr. Hudson?"

I punched his upper arm. "Right now, Mr. Hudson."

We were still laughing when the police car pulled up.

Nick and Diane got out of the back, two uniformed officers out of the front.

This was not a social call.

"Nick?" I asked worriedly.

"We're here on business, Ashley," he said crisply.

"I can see that. Do you know Willie Hudson?"

Nick nodded. "I do know Willie. How you doin', Mr. Hudson?"

"Fine, sir. And yourself?"

"Is Miss Talliere here?" Diane asked.

The two uniformed officers stood at attention near the car.

"I'll get her," I said. I walked along the colonnade to the side piazza, and into Tiffany's living quarters. "Tiffany," I called, "you here?"

Tiffany came out of her room, dressed in shorts and a tee shirt. "Oh, hi, Ashley. I was going to come find you."

My face must have shown my alarm because she asked, "Anything wrong?"

"The police are here. They want to see you."

"Sure. Guess they have some more questions."

We started out but Nick and Diane had followed, the two police officers behind them.

"What is . . .?" Tiffany started to ask.

"Tiffany Talliere," Diane said, "we have a warrant for your arrest. We are charging you with the murder of Mindy Chesterton."

"No!" I cried.

Tiffany was speechless; her mouth had dropped open.

The two officers started forward with handcuffs.

Diane continued, "I have to advise you of your rights. You have the right to remain silent. If you give up the right to silence, anything you say can, and will, be used against you in a court of law.

"You have a right to an attorney. If you cannot afford an attorney, one will be provided for you by the court. Do you understand these rights as I've explained them to you?"

Tiffany, eyes wide, nodded. "Yes."

"Good, then let's go."

Tiffany stood docilely as one officer cuffed her hands behind her back.

Taking her by the elbow, Diane led her across the colonnade, down the steps, and to the waiting police car. She even did the thing with the hand on the head, so Tiffany wouldn't bump her head.

Gus raced out the front door. "Someone said . . . Tiffany!"

He ran to the car. One of the officers intercepted him. "Stand back."

Gus backed off. He turned to Nick who stood with me on the steps. "What's going on? Where are you taking Tiffany?"

Nick explained about the arrest as Diane got into the police car. She was sending Nick impatient looks.

"I've got to go."

"Nick! Wait!" I said. "Why have you arrested her?"

"Arrested!" Gus blurted.

"There were only three sets of fingerprints on the glass that contained the poison," Nick said. "Miss Chesterton's, the EMT's, and Miss Talliere's."

"But . . ."

Nick raised a hand. "If Elaine McDuff had prepared the tea as Miss Talliere says she did, her prints should have been on the glass too. But they are not. And we have witnesses who can testify that they heard Miss Talliere threaten to kill Miss Chesterton."

"But . . ."

"Ashley, I've got to go." He looked at Gus. "Call a lawyer for her."

Gus ran to the police car, hollered to Tiffany through the window, "Don't worry, Tiffany. I'm getting a lawyer for you. We'll meet you there."

25

"Another glass of wine, Ashley?" Gus offered. We were back at Moon Gate after a long, exhausting day of first hiring a defense attorney then driving to police headquarters to meet him there. Naturally I had gone with Gus. I no longer thought of Tiffany and Gus as clients, I thought of them as friends.

He'd also called Cameron Jordan, and I'd called Melanie. Cam had promised to help, and so had Melanie.

While work progressed on the house, Gus and I had driven to town and back. Now in the early evening, the crews were breaking up, loading tools into their trucks and taking off. Jon and Willie had left earlier for Jon's office to do some planning on the new computer program. Jon was as concerned about Tiffany as I was, but we'd agreed that one of us had to manage the project, and he'd volunteered.

So all of a sudden, the house was quiet. And all too soon we were into the second bottle of wine. My feet were propped up on the coffee table. I was winding down and maybe a little tipsy.

"I know she didn't do it," I said. "They'll have to let her off."

"Of course, she didn't do it. My little sister is gentle and kind. Murder? Impossible."

"I can't believe I've known you and Tiffany for only a week. I feel like I know you so well."

"Same for me," Gus replied. "And I know Tiff feels the same."

Gus had been traveling when I'd first met Tiffany. "What did you study at Duke?" I asked, recalling that he had a master's degree from Duke University.

"Earth science," he replied, propping his feet up across from mine. "I studied at the Nicholas School of the Environment and Earth Sciences."

"Isn't that where Orrin Pilkey teaches?" I asked. Orrin Pilkey is an expert in beach erosion and coastal management.

"Yes, my best classes were with him. And you know that fight between Caswell Beach and Oak Island with Bald Head Island about who deserved to get the re-nourishment sand was an argument without substance."

"I think I know what you mean," I said.

"We can't stop nature from changing the contour of the shorelines. Beach erosion is inevitable."

"You sound like an environmentalist."

"I am. I visited Suriname and French Guiana this spring, Ashley, and I learned first hand how people can live with nature, not live opposed to nature—fighting it all the time. Let me start dinner and I'll tell you about it."

"I'd like to hear. And I'd like to help with dinner." I lowered my feet to the floor.

"No, you're the guest. Put your feet back up. Just sit there and relax. The beauty of this one-room living is that I can talk to you while I cook. I'll prepare a native dish for you, *Saramakan* Chicken. And we'll drink Konsa with it. *Konsa* is a beverage made of fermented sugarcane."

Gus filled a dutch oven with water and set it to boil. As it heated, he removed two chicken breasts from the refrigerator and two roots from a bin.

"Cassava root and taro root," he said.

He began chopping the roots.

I like a man who knows his way around a kitchen. I don't know how to cook but I've decided to learn. Recently, I bought a collection of recipes called *Modern Recipes From Historic Wilmington*,published by the Lower Cape Fear Historical Society. My goal is to master one recipe a week.

"I visited Kaw, an almost inaccessible wildlife area. The abundant marshes at Kaw are home to a variety of birds I've never seen before. So colorful, so exotic. And home of caimans—small alligators."

The chicken was simmering with the roots, smelling wonderful. Suddenly, I realized I was hungry.

Gus carried the bottle of red wine to me and refilled my glass. Then he went back behind the counter, measured rice and peanuts, and added them to the pot.

"I visited the remote village of the Saramaka and went on a *ponsu* with them. That's where I learned to make this dish."

"What's a *ponsu*?" I asked, sipping my wine.

"A *ponsu* is a fishing event that the Saramaka learned from older, indigenous tribes. They take special herbs, sprinkle them on the lake. The fish eat the herbs and become drugged, barely able to move. Then it's just a matter of spreading the nets. The fish won't swim away."

"But wouldn't the drugs hurt the people when they ate the fish?"

"Not in such minute quantities. I think our dinner is ready. Set the silverware for us, will you?"

I laid the table, and Gus served the meal. It was delicious, a taste I'd never experienced. With it, we drank the *Konsa*, a sweet drink with a strong taste that reminded me of *sake*.

Gus cleared the table. "I'll just load the dishwasher. Why don't you relax on the sofa. This will just take a moment."

I leaned my head on the sofa pillow and must have dozed off because the next thing I knew I awoke to the sound of the shower running in the bathroom.

How embarrassing. I'd passed out like a common drunk. I got up and tore a sheet of paper off a yellow pad and scribbled a note of thanks and apology to Gus.

Then I hightailed it out of there, feeling slightly woozy but sober enough to drive. Ashley Wilkes, Southern belle, lady of refinement, falls asleep on host's sofa. I hoped I hadn't snored.

26

On Thursday evening after a good day's work on Moon Gate, and after receiving news that Tiffany had been released on bail, then seeing her arrive home, I drove into Melanie's heavily wooded neighborhood off Greenville Loop Road. Gus hadn't said a word about my falling asleep on his sofa, and for that I was grateful.

Melanie's house is at the end of Rabbit Run on Sandpiper Cove, a sprawling ranch with bleached cedar shakes, green shutters, and a split rail fence that was covered with early-blooming wild roses.

My headlights picked out the opening in the fence and I maneuvered my Alero down her sloping, sandy driveway, pulling into the last available spot.

The house was lit up like a cruise ship, and music flowed out into the yard. I took my purse and stepped carefully down illuminated shallow steps to her small front porch. Pressing the doorbell, I heard soft chimes play inside.

Cameron opened the door quickly and let me in. My feet sank into thick carpet as I stepped inside the foyer.

"Hi there, Ashley," he said. "The guest of honor has not yet arrived, and Melanie has worked herself into one hell of a snit."

The guest of honor was Clay Aiken who was performing tonight at a sold-out concert at Thalian Hall. Melanie had arranged a pre-concert party in his honor. Clay Aiken was from Raleigh, and a recent graduate of UNC-Charlotte. His album "Measure of a Man" was a huge hit; he'd starred on network specials, on MTV, appeared on The Tonight Show, and was just the biggest thing that had happened to North Carolina since John Edwards!

Cameron took my jacket. Melanie is always so fabulously turned out that I had taken pains with my outfit too. Blues and pinks are my best colors. I had on a simple sheath in a deep rose with a matching jacket that Cameron was now holding over his arm.

He moved me into the living room. Stepping inside, I thought back to how Melanie and I had decorated this room together when I was home from Parsons School of Design one summer. How much fun we'd had shopping for the wonderful art deco pieces that blended marvelously with the fat Thirties-style Tuxedo sofas and club chairs. How we'd selected the filmy linen panels that hung in deep folds across the sliding glass doors that led to the terrace. Everything here was serene, done in pale taupes and ivories with deft touches of peach and aqua.

"Oh!" I exclaimed, and my hand went out to Cameron's arm. "The new painting is marvelous over the fireplace!"

Somehow the striking hot colors of the painting complimented the quietly cool room perfectly. The painting became the focal point and all eyes were drawn to it.

Something warm and furry wrapped around my ankle and I reached down to pick up Spunky. I rubbed his cheek against mine and he purred deeply. "So you do remember me, you little traitor," I teased.

He gave me a long, level, cat-eyed look, almost as if he understood every word and would reply if the subject were not just too trivial, and not really worth the effort. Cats!

"He follows Melanie around this house, never lets her out of his sight," Cameron said. "You'd think he was a dog."

"He's an ungrateful beast, is what he is," I said. "I'm the one who rescued him from cold and starvation. And who does he fall for? Like most men, Melanie!"

Cameron chuckled.

"Cameron," I said, setting Spunky back down gently on his feet, "they let Tiffany out on bail this morning. She said your studio posted bail for her. That was so good of you."

"I know Tiffany didn't kill Mindy. It's all a mistake. The police will find the real killer, then Tiffany will be off the hook. Till then, I'm going to do everything in my power to exonerate her, and to show the world that I and the studio have faith in her. And I'm doing that by keeping her on the show."

"Melanie's a lucky girl. You're a gem," I said, smiling up at him—he was over six feet tall—feeling a good mood coming on, until I was brought up short by the sight of Mickey Ballantine mingling with the other guests.

Oh, Melanie, you sure do like living on the edge.

"Nick said he'd try to make it," I told Cameron. "Is he here?"

"Hasn't put in an appearance yet, Ashley. And I'm minding the door, so I should know."

The doorbell chimed. "See what I mean," he said with a grin. "Excuse me."

Where was Melanie? I started into the dining room when Mickey Ballantine intercepted me.

"Hello again, Miss Wilkes."

"Call me Ashley," I said. "I was just on my way to find Melanie."

He gave me his hand. "If you'll call me Mickey. I think Melanie is in the kitchen with the caterer. I trust there were no problems associated with your unfortunate accident."

I shrugged. Did he know about the brick that had been thrown through my window, or about the threatening note? How often did Melanie see him? And what might she have told him about me?

"Just a dented tail gate. The car's old, it's not worth fixing," I said casually.

Mickey had on another of his black-on-black ensembles. "Well, if you ever decide you want to have it repaired, I've got a repair shop can fix it up good as new for you."

"Why, thank you, Mr. Ba . . . Mickey. But I thought you were in the nightclub business."

"I got my fingers in lots of pies, Ashley. Diversified, that's the way to succeed these days."

"Yes," I replied, remembering that the officer who had written up the report on Melanie's stolen Jaguar said something about a chop-shop. I also recalled that Heather Thorp and Brook Cole thought Mickey was attractive. Not to me. Reptilian was the description that came to my mind.

Mickey looked away from me, across the room. His expression conveyed consuming interest. I turned and saw Melanie striding toward us.

"Nice party," Mickey told her.

"Thanks, Mickey." Melanie purred just like Spunky. No wonder they adored each other. "Has Cam taken care of you? Does your drink need refreshing?"

He lifted his half full glass. "I'm fine, Melanie. You're looking beautiful tonight."

She did look spectacular in an off-white dress, strapless and short, with gold high-heeled strappy sandals.

"Could I see you for a moment in the kitchen?" she said to me, her tone for her one-and-only sister totally devoid of syrup.

"Sure," I said and followed her through the noisy crowd into the kitchen.

I hadn't thought about whom she might hire to cater the party but I really wasn't surprised to see Elaine there. Melanie and Elaine had gone to high school together, had been in home-room together, Melanie told me, and if Melanie likes you, she likes you, and is loyal and affectionate. And she liked Elaine.

Elaine stopped filling mushroom caps and said, "Hi, Ashley."

"Elaine, I'm so sorry about Larry," I said.

"The flowers you sent were appreciated, Ashley."

"Elaine and I want to talk to you about something important," Melanie explained. "But not here. Back in my bedroom."

I followed the two of them down the carpeted hallway and into the master bedroom suite with Spunky trailing behind us. Melanie's bedroom could have been a set for a Thirties' movie, everything white and satiny, with pale blonde art deco furniture. Spunky jumped into the center of the bed.

Even though whatever they had to discuss with me had to do with Elaine, Melanie couldn't repress her disappointment that Clay Aiken was late. "If he doesn't show, I'll be so humiliated I'll never be able to show my face in this town again."

Elaine sank down onto the foot of the Hollywood bed with her and patted her shoulder. "He'll be here. It's still early."

"Elaine, how are you getting along?" I asked.

She dropped her head. "I get through the days okay, Ashley. My work keeps me busy. But the nights, forget it. I haven't slept in two nights. I don't know which is worse, thinking he committed suicide, or knowing someone killed him. But why?" she asked, her soft round face twisted with grief, and something more, outrage.

Melanie wrapped her arm around Elaine. "The police will get whoever did this. Ashley's dating the best homicide detective we have on the Wilmington force; he'll get Larry's killer."

She looked at me over Elaine's bent head. "And that's why we want to talk to you, shug. Elaine has a favor to ask you. Go ahead, honey bunch, tell Ashley what you told me."

Elaine hesitated a moment.

"It's okay, Elaine, you can trust Ashley. She can keep a secret. She'd better if she wants to stay my sister."

Elaine sized me up thoughtfully. I dragged a chair away from Melanie's dressing table and pulled it up close to them.

"Okay," she sighed. "I'm going to tell you something but I don't want what I say to leave this room. Do you agree?"

I looked from Melanie to Elaine. "Sure," I said. "What is it?"

"Look, Ashley, this is delicate." She reached into her pocket and pulled out a pack of cigarettes. "I know you don't like smoking in your house, Melanie, but I've gotta have this."

Melanie arched her eyebrows. "Sure," she said, and got up, rummaged around in the dressing table drawer and produced an ashtray.

After Elaine inhaled deeply, and I squinted through the smoke, she said, "Ashley, I found a lot of money. Cash. Hidden in an old suitcase in Larry's closet. I was going through his things, selecting a suit for him to be buried in, and wondering if I'd ever have the heart to give his things to Goodwill, so I pulled down this old suitcase for his shoes and stuff, thinking if I never got it back that'd be okay."

She took another puff on the cigarette, and Melanie fanned the air in front of her face.

"It's funny the things you think about at a time like this."

"Not so funny," I said. "I remember the trivial stuff we got involved with when Daddy died. Remember, Mel. We couldn't decide if it was disrespectful to leave the Christmas tree up, and you, me, and Mama had a long discussion about it. Finally, we just left it up because we didn't have the energy to take it down. So I know what you mean,

Elaine. When is the funeral, by the way?"

"Tomorrow. Oh, I know, people'll criticize me for being here tonight, but what do I care? What did they ever do for me?"

"That's the spirit," Melanie said. "Now tell Ashley about the money, and what you want her to do about it."

"Me? Do about . . . "

"Shhh," Melanie said, a finger to her lips. "Go ahead, Elaine."

"Well, I dragged down this old suitcase, and when I opened it up, it was stuffed with money. I swear, Ashley, I almost fainted."

She dragged on the cigarette again. "I counted it. Almost two hundred thousand dollars. Where'd Larry get that kind of money? And why was he hiding it?"

I shook my head. "I don't know what to say, Elaine."

"Well, obviously, it has something to do with why he was killed," Melanie said.

"I think so too," Elaine said, stabbing out the cigarette in the ashtray. Thank you Lord for small favors.

"If you think that, you should turn the money over to the police," I said.

"That's just what we want to talk to you about, shug. You see, Elaine needs that money."

"I do, Ashley. I'm just making it in this business. My costs are going up and with Larry gone, I'll have to hire an assistant. But, here's the thing. If I turn the money over to the police, will they give it back to me? After they solve the crime, I mean."

"Well . . ."

Melanie broke in. "That's what we want you to find out, shug. We want you to pose a hypothetical question to Nick. Tell him you were just wondering what happens to found cash. Does it get returned to the person who found it? Get him all lovey dovey and then spring it on him; he'll tell you and not even remember that he did."

"But if the cash was part of a crime . . ." I began. "If Larry got it through illegal means, then it would have to be returned to the real owner."

"Larry would never do anything illegal!" Elaine said vehemently. "He wasn't that kind of person."

"I'd like to help, Elaine, honestly I would, but I just don't think I could fool Nick that way. Besides I don't think it would work. He's sharp; he'll see right through me."

"Are you refusing to help poor Elaine?" Melanie declared, mad as the dickens.

I looked at her helplessly. "I can't, Mel. I just can't. Look, you haven't thought this through. Either of you. You've just said you think that money had something to do with Larry being killed, so, Elaine, you could be in danger if you keep it. You need to turn that money over to the police. Get rid of it."

They looked at each other. "We don't really know it's the reason Larry was killed," Melanie said. "But, Elaine, we sure don't want you put at risk."

"Oh, jeez. I don't know what to do," Elaine cried.

I got up. "Well, let me know if you want me to tell Nick about it, pave the way for you."

"Ashley Wilkes, you are not to say a word about this to anyone, do you hear me?"

"Didn't I promise not to? Honestly, Melanie, you'd think I was a person who can't keep her word."

"Well, see that you do. Elaine and I have got to figure this out.

"Maybe," she said, turning to Elaine, "we could get someone to keep an eye on you till the case is solved. I'm sure Mickey would know someone reliable."

Mickey again, I thought, as I left them with their heads together, plotting. Foolishness, was what I thought about it.

The first person I bumped into when I fled into the dining room was Nick. "Sweetheart, I've been looking all over for you. Aiken's just pulling up outside in one of those party buses like you wouldn't believe. You okay?"

"Why wouldn't I be?" I asked, feeling like he knew exactly what the three of us had been plotting.

We spent most of the party on the sofa, holding hands, just being quiet. It gave me time to think. Larry had left a large of amount of cash; Mindy was being blackmailed. Didn't take a genius to put that together. I gave Nick a surreptitious look. I certainly hoped Elaine would turn the money over to the police. If I could put it together, so would they.

And how extraordinary: Larry's funeral and Mindy's funeral on the same day.

When it was time to leave for the drive downtown to Thalian Hall, I drove my car and Nick followed me in his.

We held hands through the concert which was so good I felt like signing on to become one of Clay's "Claymates," but quickly dismissed that idea when Nick said he was following me home and spending the night. Nick was the only one I wanted to "mate" with.

As we turned the corner into Nun Street, it was *deja vu* all over again, a blue and white Wilmington PD cruiser parked in front of my house, my burglar alarm shattering the peace of the neighborhood. Only a few heads peered out of windows and I assumed that like me my neighbors were returning from the concert.

Nick assumed his cop's mantle as we marched up onto my porch, greeting the officers curtly by name, taking charge.

"Kitchen door's been broken in, Nick," an officer said. "Someone took a crowbar to the lock. Whoever did it is gone. Get her to turn that noisy thing off."

I unlocked the front door with my key and turned off the howling alarm system.

"What good is this thing?" I demanded, feeling frustrated with hot tears forming. "It doesn't prevent break-ins."

"He'd only have a few minutes, so if he knew exactly what he was after, he'd find it and be gone. We don't have wings, you know. It takes a few minutes to get a squad car here."

Nick was frustrated too. "Let's take a look and see what's missing."

We found the damage in the library. My desk had been ransacked, drawers pulled out, the contents tossed on the floor.

"My laptop is gone!" I cried.

Nick gave me a searching look. "Why would someone steal your laptop? What do you have on it?"

Guilt made me break out in a sweat, yet I did my best to look innocent. How I hated lying to Nick. "Just business stuff," I said, but I knew someone was after the compact disk with the pictures of Mindy, and the blurred image of the man.

Nick's fear made him angry. "Someone thinks you know something about Mindy's murder."

He grabbed me squarely by the shoulders and made me look him in the eye. "Do you know something, Ashley?"

To lie to him again would kill me. So I did exactly what I felt like doing—I wept.

He pulled my head onto his shoulder and wrapped his arms around me. "Don't cry, baby. You know I can't stand to see you cry. I'm going to get this guy and nail his hide to the courthouse door."

27

Late Friday afternoon, after Willie and the crews left Moon Gate for a weekend off, Jon and I were on our way to our makeshift porch office to review next week's projects, and to go over materials lists. Passing through the sitting room, we found Gus glued to the television set. From the look on his face and the excitement in the TV reporter's voice, something earth-shaking had happened.

"What is it?" I asked anxiously. "Not another terrorist attack?"

Pulling up a chair next to Gus, I stared at the screen. The broadcast was local: TV cameras were aimed from the State Port out across the Cape Fear to the dredging arena.

Because of budgetary constraints, the Harbor Deepening Project had not been completed by the end of last year as planned. Then the federal government appropriated $17.5 million for the project and it was carried over into the new year with completion scheduled for the spring—now. When complete the navigation channel would be deepened from 38 feet to 42, allowing larger and heavier ships to enter the port.

"What's going on?" I asked Gus again.

"Shut up and listen," he snarled.

I glanced up at Jon who raised his eyebrows. *Uh oh, he's in a foul mood*, his look seemed to say.

Jon handed me an icy Coke from the refrigerator, and took one for himself. At the risk of another reprimand, I popped the tab and quenched my dusty throat with a long swallow.

Gus looked at me. "I'm sorry, Ashley, I shouldn't have snapped at you. They've found something in the river. The dredging was halted this morning when they encountered something down there. The Army Corps of Engineers brought in multibeam and side-scan sonar equipment, and they've found what they think is a wrecked ship. So they sent divers down to investigate; they've been in and out all day."

I zoned in on the TV screen. The camera crew and reporters were on board a launch out on the Cape Fear as near to the dredging arena as the Coast Guard would allow.

The camera panned the area. There were the two dredges, and the barge they'd been loading, and another ship which must have been the high-tech equipment ship the Army Corps brought in.

All fall and winter, I'd read about the progress of the dredging project in the *Star-News*. The larger dredge was a suction dredge, faster and more efficient than the smaller dredge, but because of environmental concerns—things like turtle nesting, for example—had to be operated carefully and infrequently.

The smaller dredge had a scoop mechanism on it, and it scooped up sand from the river and deposited it on barges. Then the barges transported the re-nourishment sand downriver to Bald Head Island's South Beach.

"You would have thought if there was a wrecked vessel out there, the Army Corps would have known about it," Jon said.

"Not necessarily," Gus argued. "And not if it was small. With the number of hurricanes we get, the river bottom might have shifted, burying the vessel in sand, then shifted again to expose it. More likely the dredging exposed it."

"Do you think . . . " Jon began.

Gus raised a warning hand. "Listen!"

The news reporter's face filled the screen, the view of the Cape Fear and the dredging arena a backdrop.

"This news just in. A spokesperson for the Coast Guard has confirmed that the sunken ship is a two-masted schooner. Schooners and sloops were the two most common vessels to ply the Cape Fear in the 1800s. They were used as fishing vessels and for transporting freight. More schooners were constructed in the Wilmington shipyards than any other vessel.

"And divers were able to verify that the name of this particular schooner was 'The Lucy.'"

Gus leapt out of his chair, startling me so badly I dropped my Coke can. The caramel liquid spread over the floor.

The television reporter was saying, "Archaeologists will have to research this particular ship before any information about its owner and history can be determined. There is a cargo hold, and a second team of divers has gone down to explore it."

I moved to the sink to find a sponge, wanting to sop up the Coke before it dried and became sticky.

I stopped when I saw Gus. He looked like he was about to have a heart attack. His face was bright red, his eyes were popping wide; in a minute he'd be foaming at the mouth.

At the same time, Jon asked, "Say, wasn't Caesar's wife's name Lucy?"

With that Gus let out an agonizing howl, like he was in pain. I backed up against the sink. Caesar's ship? Could it be?

Gus's eyes were rivetted to the TV screen and he grabbed up the remote control to increase the volume.

I tiptoed around to a spot behind him from where I could see the screen.

The news reporter was facing toward the dredging arena so that all we saw of him was the back of his head. Then he turned, his hand pressed to the earphone tucked into his ear. A look of great excitement crossed his face.

"Folks, there's startling news. Divers have broken into the cargo hold where they discovered human remains. A skull was found, along with human bones. We can say with certainty that a human being was on board that ship when it went down. We can only speculate on how this person came to be locked in the cargo hold.

"It appears that the hull was smashed so that the ship was deliberately scuttled leaving . . ."

Gus was up out of his chair again, literally tearing his hair out of his head. "I knew it! I knew it!" he exploded. "Caesar wrote about them in his journal. They killed him. I've always known they killed him. I just didn't know how."

He was pacing wildly about the small room, bumping into furniture, flailing his arms and hurling objects onto the floor.

Jon approached him, placed a hand on his shoulder. "Gus, what can we do for you? Would you like to sit down, buddy, talk about it? Can I get you a drink?"

"Just get out!" he roared. "Get the hell out!"

28

"We used to live here during the war," Aunt Ruby said. "Claire, do you remember?"

"I remember *Lumina*," Mama said.

Aunt Ruby was older than Mama but it didn't show. Mama would always be pretty, but she'd aged a lot because of her illness. Now the doctors had discovered that by combining two of the drugs used for treating early Alzheimer's, they were having good success with some of their patients. And happily for our family, Mama was one of the success stories.

Oh, we all knew that eventually she'd have to go back to the nursing home, but for now she could live at home. And dear Aunt Ruby, God bless her, had agreed to take Mama home to Savannah.

Aunt Ruby was a retired registered nurse, in her early seventies, but a role model for us all. She was vibrant and active, laced up her Reeboks every day, rain or shine, and walked for two miles, wore make-up and colored her hair.

Binkie was smitten. He couldn't take his eyes off her.

We were having dinner at Bluewater, out on the Intracoastal Waterway. The evening was summer-like so we'd voted to sit out on the deck at a large round table with room enough for all of us. There was

Mama and Aunt Ruby, Binkie, Melanie and Cameron, Nick and his sweetheart—me.

"I didn't know that you lived in Wilmington as girls," I said. "I thought you grew up in Savannah."

"We did live mostly in Savannah, Ashley," Aunt Ruby said. "But during the war years Daddy—your grandaddy—worked up here for a while. He was valuable to the war effort as a shipyard foreman. Of course, we had naval yards in Savannah too, but Daddy went where he was needed. And where Daddy went, Mama went, and we girls too."

A yacht had cruised up to the dock, and the yacht owners had disembarked to come up the boardwalk and be seated at the table next to ours on the deck. I couldn't help staring; what a fabulous life style.

Nick noticed. "Envious?" he inquired softly so no one else could hear. "I can't offer you a yacht. Will a houseboat do?"

I whispered back, "Anywhere you are, sweetheart. I'm glad you could make it tonight. It means a lot to me to have you here with my family."

"I know, and that's why I told them down at the station they'd have to get along without me for a few hours. But I'm afraid I've got to go back just as soon as dinner's over."

I wanted to ask him for details about the discovery of the sunken ship, ask him if the police, or the Coast Guard, or whoever handled such things, had verified that it was indeed Caesar Talliere's missing schooner, and if they thought the bones were Caesar's. But this was not the time.

"Do you remember when we first met, Ruby?" Binkie inquired hopefully.

"I shall never forget, Benjamin." She turned to all of us. "Benjamin and I met at the Children's Dance at Lumina Pavilion. Claire, you were there too, but you were such a little thing."

"I loved the music," Mama said meekly. She was rather subdued and quiet, but she was here, in mind and in body, and that was all that counted.

"Oh, the music," Aunt Ruby reminisced. "Jimmy Dorsey, Kay Kyser, the great band leaders all came to *Lumina*. And once a week, there would be a children's dance.

"But at other times, during the summer months, we children would be allowed to play outside on the beach and watch the grown-ups dance."

"And don't forget," Binkie reminded, his eyes twinkling merrily, "watch for German submarines."

"Oh, I do remember that. How much I wanted to see one, but I never did."

"And then the black-out came," Binkie said, "and all those brilliant lights—hundreds of incandescent lights—had to be turned off, and *Lumina* closed until the war was over.

"And after the war, you and Claire returned to Savannah with your parents," he said sadly. "How I missed you. You were the cat's meow, as we used to say. And a whiz at the fox-trot."

"As I recall, so were you, Benjamin. And we did correspond," Aunt Ruby said wistfully. "And I never married. Did you?"

"No, Ruby, I never found anyone to compare with my dancing partner," Binkie confessed.

They smiled happily at each other across the table.

The waiter took our drink orders, and some of us had wine, others iced tea.

Melanie and Cameron had been listening to this exchange, and Melanie both surprised and pleased me when she said, "Binkie, Ashley and I will be driving to Savannah often to visit Mama. Why don't you plan to come with us as often as you can."

"I'd like that, Melanie. Ruby, what do you think? Shall I come?"

Aunt Ruby smiled broadly. "I'd love for you to see our family home and to spend some time there with us. Good suggestion, Melanie."

"How're things going with the show?" Nick asked Cameron. "Have your stars recovered from their injuries? That was some free-for-all, I heard."

"I was there," I said. "I saw it. How do you manage those guys, Cam?"

"Believe or not, on the set, they're one hundred percent professionals. Off the set, they act like kids. Actually, even bad publicity is good publicity; it's better than being ignored. We've gotten a lot of calls and e-mails from fans wishing them well.

"No bones were broken, just a lot of bruises and shiners. The writers wrote their bruises into Monday's episode. In the script, the guys had a run-in with some obnoxious jocks. We made the whole thing work for us."

Melanie snuggled near him. "That's because you're a genius, darling."

"Well, what really happened?" Nick asked. "Was it a fight in earnest. I heard they were fighting about Mindy's death. Joey Fielding accused Jimmy Ryder of being responsible. The cops on the scene said the fight looked like the real thing to them. But then no one was willing to press charges."

"They told me they were just horsing around," Cameron replied. "Boys will be boys, that sort of thing. They were upset about Mindy's death and had too much to drink."

"I see," Nick said doubtfully.

The waiter returned to our table, pad and pencil in hand, and took our orders. Nick and I decided to share the Caribbean platter—coconut shrimp, chicken, island crab. The others ordered house specialties, fresh catch, roasted chicken. The cuisine was casual American, something for everyone.

Twilight on the waterway was spectacularly beautiful with dusk settling in along the shores, lights twinkling on.

"What do the police know about that sunken ship that was recovered today?" Cameron asked Nick.

I'd been hoping the subject would not come up. For one thing, I knew how much Nick disliked discussing ongoing investigations. For another, I worried that subjects like this might disturb Mama, but she seemed engrossed with the fish platter the waiter had set before her.

Nick waited until all our plates had been served before saying, "The state archaeologists are investigating. That's about all I know, Cameron."

But I felt sure he knew far more than he was telling. I suspected Cameron realized Nick was stalling, although there was nothing further he could say.

"I hear Nem Chesterton is running for mayor," Aunt Ruby said. "I used to be good friends with his wife's mother when we were girls."

"Janet's mother?" I asked.

"Yes, we lived across the street from the family. She and I never lost touch. I recall that she didn't approve when Janet accepted Nem's proposal. She felt the Chestertons were pretentious. Telling everyone they were descended from one of Wilmington's founding families, when everyone knew the first Nehemiah Chesterton was nothing more than a carpetbagger—an opportunist of the worse sort."

"I never knew that," I said. "Why would someone make up a story like that?"

"Why to build themselves up," Mama replied demurely.

"Did you know this?" I asked, turning to Binkie.

"Why, yes, Ashley dear. I thought we discussed it last Sunday while we were having lunch at the Pilot House. We had a long talk about the Reconstruction period."

"No, you only told me about Caesar Talliere's history, not about the original Nehemiah Chesterton. What's the story on him?"

Binkie put down his fork. "He was not a gentleman, Ashley, nor was he an ethical man. He was an unscrupulous opportunist, just as Ruby says. He saw a chance to seize a shipyard and he took it. The owner had been killed at Vicksburg. His widow was desperate. Chesterton bought the shipyard for pennies on the dollar, virtually stole it from her."

"And if I remember my local history correctly, Benjamin," Aunt Ruby interjected, "he was in direct competition with Caesar Talliere. They were both vying for lucrative steamship contracts. Then when Talliere disappeared, Chesterton's shipyard got the work."

I didn't feel this conversation should go any further with Mama sitting there taking it all in. There was the possibility she'd find it upsetting and I had to protect her. I let the matter drop.

But I did recall my conversation with Binkie and how he'd told me that in a bitter backlash against the gains blacks were making in the areas of politics and economics, segregationists and White Supremacists had launched a vicious campaign to intimidate them, a campaign that included beatings and disappearances of so-called troublemakers in the night.

So Gus might be right, I thought.

Nick sensed my reservations and the need to change the subject, for he said loudly, "Anyone for dessert?"

Later, when I drove Mama and Aunt Ruby back to my house, we found a box of roses left on my front porch. *Ashley*, the note read, *Please forgive my boorish behavior and please continue your fine work on Moon Gate. Gus.*

29

On Saturday afternoon after I saw Mama and Aunt Ruby on their way to Savannah, Jon picked me up and we drove down River Road to Moon Gate. Willie and his crews were off for the day, but their absence would provide Jon and me a chance to evaluate the week's progress.

All week, Willie's roofers had been up on the roof, replacing missing slate tiles, while another crew had tackled the broken window panes. The panes had been removed and in many instances, window frames that were badly rotten or warped had been pulled out too. New templates were being made, and from them custom window frames would be constructed. Now many of the window apertures were covered with plywood to keep out the weather.

We found Gus in the front parlor, applying the heat plate to painted trim, causing it to soften and blister; then he'd scrape it off. Between the two front floor-to-ceiling windows, a murky pier glass reflected wavering reflections of the three of us.

I shot Jon a frustrated look that said, *I told him not to do this.* But Gus owned the house; what else could we do but ask nicely?

"Gus," I said, trying to keep my tone pleasant, "we have professionals who can do that. You don't need to be wasting your time with it. Surely, you have better things to do."

Gus cast me a bitter stare. "It helps to keep busy. I've got to do something, and working with my hands keeps me occupied."

He stood the plate in a safe upright position. "They haven't confirmed that the remains are Caesar's but I know they are. It was his schooner; 'Lucy' was etched into the prow. He disappeared without a trace. Now we know why."

"We're sorry, Gus," Jon said.

"I hate it that this is happening to you and Tiffany," I said.

"Oh, Tiffany," he said with disgust. "She's on the set. All she cares about is that ridiculous show. Well, at least you guys came. Thanks for that."

He picked up a scraper and began scraping off the softened paint. "I'd better get back to this."

"We'll be upstairs if you need us," I said.

Jon hefted his camera case and hoisted the strap over his shoulder. In Caesar's room, he turned on the overhead light, then unpacked the $25,000 35mm camera.

"You're like a kid with a toy," I said.

"Well, this new computer program is great, but I'm just getting the hang of it. I need more shots of this room, the bathroom and the chase, then tomorrow I'll load the data into the computer. The program will automatically measure the space and produce drawings."

"Okay, have your fun," I laughed. "I'm going to stroll down to the carriage house. Tiffany asked me to take a look at it. She'd like us to convert it into a guest house."

"Um hmm," Jon said, distracted, peering down into the view finder.

"You aren't listening," I said.

"Yes, I am. I'll join you down there in a while. I can take pictures of the carriage house and the computer will measure everything and produce drawings. This'll be good practice."

I laughed. "You really are having fun with that thing, aren't you?"

"Sure, it's fun, but it's also a good investment. This will save us time, it's accurate, and it's a deductible business expense.

"Which leads me to something I've been thinking about," he continued. "You and I have been working together informally for over a year now. How about if we make our arrangement formal, set up a partnership?"

I was so touched I wanted to kiss him.

"Jon, I'm flattered. That someone of your stature would want to be my partner—well, you've made me very happy. Yes, I'd be delighted to be your partner."

"Okay, we'll catch some dinner later and talk about how we want to set things up. Then we'll find a lawyer to make it all legal."

I grinned, and threw my arms around him.

"Hey, watch the camera," he cried, but chuckled.

I backed off. "Think I'll check on Gus on my way out."

As I passed the broad archway to the front parlor, I called to Gus, "I'm going down to the carriage house for a look around."

He was working like one possessed. Not even bothering to glance my way, he mumbled, "Okay," over his shoulder.

"Be sure to unplug that thing when you aren't using it."

He grumbled something I didn't catch, and I left.

It was about five o'clock and the shadows were lengthening, but it was still clear and sunny, a really pretty day. I followed a walkway that led away from the house, toward the carriage house. Azaleas bordered the walk, and live oaks arched overhead. Birds sang, and in the distance the river lapped gently against the pilings under the boat dock. What a heavenly place, I thought, as I walked. I really couldn't fault Gus for being obsessed with his ancestral home.

The carriage house was in worse condition than the house, if that was possible, and I knew I wouldn't be able to make a judgement about its soundness without Jon's input. But I could get a general overall impression about the feasibility of Tiffany's plan. Tugging on one of a pair of doors, I dragged it open. The other stuck on the ground so I stepped around inside and pushed it outward.

The carriage house was dim inside but when I threw open the doors the western sun flooded the interior with light. There was another set of doors but I didn't bother with them.

All sorts of odds and ends had been dumped in here, and an old truck was parked inside too.

I felt a happy glow at the thought of Jon's invitation that we form a partnership. He was such a great guy, so good at what he did, a valuable friend. We were a good team, and a formal partnership would just be icing on the cake.

I glanced up at the beamed rafters, thinking it would be nice to leave them exposed, then swept my gaze around the space, trying to picture a kitchenette at one end, a bathroom and dressing room at the other, a great room in between.

But something was bothering me, and I felt off-kilter. The hairs on the back of my neck bristled and every instinct told me that something was wrong.

The truck, something about the truck. I gave it a second look. It was parked facing out; whoever had put it here—Gus?—had backed it in. And there was something familiar about it.

I had a flashback to the menacing truck that had born down on me on Airlie Road. This was that truck! I leaned in closer for a better look at the grill and the bumper. Dark blue paint streaks! Dark blue paint from my Volvo.

This could mean only one thing. The person who had run me off the road and tried to kill me had used this truck!

"Gus!" I cried. And Gus must be the man in the picture with Mindy. Then in a whisper, I said, "Gus killed Mindy."

"Yes, I did, Ashley," Gus said from behind me.

I yelped and whirled around. I tried running past him, to dodge around him, but he sprang in my direction and grabbed me. His arms holding me tight, he dragged me from the carriage house, toward the house.

"Jon!" I cried. "Jon!" We were too far from the house for him to hear me.

I felt a sharp whack on the back of my neck, and then I felt nothing.

The sound of hammering woke me. It took me a second to get my bearings. I was lying on the floor in the sitting room of Gus and Tiffany's living quarters. My arms were bound to my side, my feet were tied, and a gag was stuffed in my mouth.

The hammering continued, coming from the second floor. I heard shouting, Jon's voice calling out, protesting, angry. What was Gus doing? With a flash I realized he was nailing the door to Caesar's room shut, possibly nailing boards across the door. Jon was sealed inside—no way out. The windows were covered with plywood.

His cell phone, I thought. He can call for help. Then I remembered he had left his cell phone in the Jeep, recharging the battery.

I started kicking furniture and succeeded in knocking over a chair. But what good did that do me?

"Calm down," Gus's voice said. I turned my head and saw him standing in the doorway to the breezeway. "Struggling will only make things worse."

"Ur, ur, ur, ur." My efforts to talk were prevented by the gag in my mouth. *Get it out*, I was trying to say. *I could choke on this damned rag.*

"If you promise not to scream, I'll remove the gag," he said in a strangely placid voice.

I nodded my head, then grasped for air when he pulled the rag out of my mouth.

"Why?" was all I whispered.

He gave me a sly smile. "You know why, Ashley. Revenge. The Chestertons destroyed my family. I won't rest until I destroy theirs."

He moved to a cabinet and took down a bottle. "Now I want you to drink this. It won't hurt you, it'll make you sleep."

He knelt beside me and put the bottle to my lips. I spit and twisted my head, and thrashed about on the floor, but it was useless. In the end, he spilled the foul liquid in my mouth, then pressed my lips together. I held it in my mouth for as long as I could, but when he forced the bottle to my lips again I had no choice but to swallow.

30

I opened my eyes and saw stars. Literally. Thousands of them, millions of them, shining down on me from a midnight sky. The moon was out too, full and glowing like a bright yellow marble, lighting up the night, reflecting off the water.

Water! I was in water, floating on the lagoon. There was the river below me, and behind and above me would be the terraced gardens and the mansion. How did I get here?

And then my memory returned in a rush. Finding the truck in the shed, Gus's admission, how he'd forced that vile liquid down my throat. Ohmygosh, it was the drug he'd told me about—the exotic herbal drug the Maroons used to drug the fish during a *ponsu*.

I tried to kick but my legs wouldn't move. My body was numb and stiff and I knew I was paralysed, just like those fish. I tried to fling out my arms, tried to stroke water with them, but all I could manage was a faint fluttering of my fingers. I had to get to shore, but how?

I tested my senses. I could see all right. And I could hear. Far up on the bluff, voices carried to me from the house—loud, excited voices; some sort of commotion going on. I opened my mouth to call to them but my voice wouldn't come.

I tried paddling with my feet, and was relieved when I felt my body wheeling about in the water. The drug must be wearing off, I thought, for life was returning to my extremities. I flipped my feet some more and found that I could rotate myself so that now I faced toward the terraced gardens and the house above.

And, oh dear God, my sense of smell was as keen as ever, for I smelled smoke, strong and acrid. Smoke burned my nostrils—smoke that was pouring out of the house. I saw flames, small at first, then great curls of them, licking out of the windows and doors and up the walls.

People were milling about without direction, shouting, calling to each other. Then came the distant screams of sirens, screams that grew more shrill as they drew nearer, until I could see the flash of lights. Fire engines and police cars roared up to the house.

Nick? Oh, Nick, are you with them? I'm down here, Nick, come get me.

But how would he ever see me down here at the bottom of the gardens?

And dear Lord, Jon! Jon was trapped inside Caesar's bedroom. He'd burn up with the house!

At the edge of the lagoon, the tall grasses rustled. Something slithered within them. Something large by the sound of the noise it made and the vibration I felt as it slipped into the water.

Oh no, dear God, the alligator! Its powerful tail hit the water with a splash, creating a wave that rippled out to me. The alligator was coming and I couldn't swim away from it.

I flipped my hands and feet frantically, the awkward motion propelling me in the opposite direction, but not nearly fast enough. The alligator was submerged in the water. All I could see of it were the horny protrusions above its eyes—eyes that were fixed on me and that did not blink, eyes that were gaining on me.

If that alligator mistook me for prey, it might eat me. And motionless as I was, it might very well suppose I was a dead animal.

Suddenly I realized this was happening just as Gus had intended it to happen: a hungry alligator, a motionless victim. He'd done it before. Those bodies that had washed up at Fort Fisher had been his victims, just as I was now. He'd drugged those men, dragged them down the hill to the lagoon, and the alligator had done the rest. Gus was a monster!

Up on the hill, in front of the house, the firefighters were dragging hoses from the tank truck. People raced about, shouting, their arms waving.

Where was Gus? Would he tell them that Jon was trapped inside the burning house? That I was floating helplessly in the lagoon with a hungry alligator?

And then I thought I saw Jon; his silhouette was so familiar to me I should know it anywhere. But were my eyes playing tricks on me? Was it really him? He was talking to another man. Nick. My Nick.

I tried to shout but all that came out was a whimper. The cry caused the alligator to pause and stare warily as it tried to decide if I was a threat or fair game. It drifted motionless toward me, only its eyes and nostrils exposed, the bumpy protrusions above its eyes aimed at me like sights down a gun barrel.

Live oaks and magnolias, hedges and flowering shrubs were obstacles between me and the house, and unless they were really looking, no one would see me down here. Still, I saw with relief that two men were hurriedly approaching, racing down through the terraced gardens, crossing the Chinese bridge to the lower end of the lagoon. Nick and Jon. Somehow they had figured out where I was. Or maybe Gus had told them.

"Hang on, Ashley!" Nick called.

"We're coming!" Jon shouted.

Nick plunged into the lagoon, waded out toward me.

Nick, I cried silently. *Hurry, Nick.*

The alligator whipped its tail and pushed its enormous snout in my direction. It was swimming swiftly now, racing with Nick to reach me first.

Nick sloughed through the water, reached out and grabbed me by the shoulders, pulling me toward the shore.

The alligator struck, powerful jaws snapping at my feet. In a flash I realized how those three unidentified young men had lost their hands and feet.

I willed myself out of its reach, willed Nick to move faster, but some vegetation must has ensnared his foot because he stopped, kicking at something in the water. Sprays gushed up as he thrashed. This seemed to excite the alligator for it aimed its snout toward Nick and swiftly closed the distance.

I couldn't bear to look. I heard Jon's shouts, then felt and heard water splashing as he waded forward to help Nick. Shots rang out, two in succession. When I opened my eyes, the alligator was thrashing its tail. With its powerful jaws pointed skyward, it rolled over on its side, and the water closed over it.

Nick holstered his pistol, then he and Jon grabbed an arm each. They raced from the water, floating me between them. When we reached the shore, Nick lifted me easily in his arms and carried me up the terraced pathways.

"It's all right, Ashley," he said soothingly. "You're safe. Don't cry, sweetheart."

I felt tears in my eyes and on my cheeks, and a pins-and-needle prickling of my skin. The drug was wearing off; my limbs were coming back to life.

The house was blazing like an inferno when we reached the top of the hill. Firefighters motioned us back. Although they trained their hoses on the house, their expressions said they had given up. There was no hope of saving it. All that old, dry wood was burning as rapidly as a pine forest after a drought.

Jon got a blanket from one of the firefighters and wrapped it around me. I opened my mouth to speak and found that I was now able. "Gus? Where's Gus?"

The three of us looked around, searching the crowd of firefighters and police officers.

"There!" I shouted. "There he is."

He was near the house, the brightness of the flames illuminating him clearly. The look on his face was stunned, disbelieving.

"Ashley!" Tiffany's voice was desperate as she came bounding toward us. "So it's true. I heard it on the news. I couldn't believe my ears." She looked at me. "You're all wet." She turned and cast her eyes about wildly, frantically. "Gus? Where's Gus? He's not . . . "

Then she saw him. "Gus," she called and started toward him. Jon grabbed her arm and drew her back.

We watched as one of the fireman approached Gus, reached out a hand to lead him to safety. But Gus brushed the hand aside, turned to the man and said something.

And then as we watched in horror, he bolted forward, raced up the steps between the tall Corinthian columns, leapt through the burning door into the flames.

Tiffany screamed. "Gus . . . oh, no!"

"Tiffany," I cried, throwing my arms around her and drawing her near, wanting to keep her close and safe.

There was a muffled roar as the roof collapsed, and the firefighters pushed us back even further away from the house. "It's all over folks," one said, but still they trained their hoses on the flames.

The skeleton of the house was pulling apart, walls tumbling inward, the second floor collapsing in a fiery blaze, crushing everything under it. Only the brick chimneys remained standing.

Tiffany looked into my face. "Oh, no . . . oh, no. He loved Caesar's house and Caesar's legends more than anything. He was . . . he was obsessed."

31

"How did you get out of that burning house?" I asked Jon.

In the wee small hours of the morning, we were settled comfortably in my library—Nick, Jon, Tiffany and me. Tiffany, homeless for the time being, was spending the night in my guest room.

I poured brandy for all of us, and enjoyed its warmth as it slid down my throat. Although I'd changed into dry clothes, the memory of floating in the lagoon at the mercy of that alligator sent shivers through me.

In answer to my question, Jon replied, "I couldn't believe it when Gus locked me in the master bedroom. Then he started hammering and I realize now he was nailing boards across the door. But then I had no idea what was up to. When I smelled smoke, I knew I had to get out of the house. Okay, so remember the small door in the bathroom that led into the chase?"

I nodded by head. Tiffany knew of it, of course, but quickly I described the function of a utility chase to Nick.

"Well, I couldn't phone for help because, if you recall, I'd left my mobile phone out in the Jeep, recharging the battery, Jon continued, "So I climbed down the chase; most of those rungs were intact. When I reached the bottom, I found the outside door locked. I had to kick it out. Good thing I'm in shape."

"Oh," I gasped, "your new camera."

He grinned. "Hung it around my neck. That baby's safe. Anyway, so I got out of the house. First thing I did was run to my Jeep to call 911, then I called Nick direct. Then I started searching for you. I didn't know where Gus had gone or what he was up to, and I'm glad we didn't cross paths. I just wanted to find you, kiddo. But just in case I did run into him, I took the precaution of removing the tire iron from the Jeep and carrying it with me for protection."

Nick said, "Diane and I were on our way out there when Jon reached me. We had an arrest warrant for Gus. The lab identified him as the man in pictures with Mindy that someone sent to Diane anonymously. And our background check on him raised some serious questions about the true source of his income. A lowlife punk was spilling his guts about drug trafficking up the Cape Fear to the Talliere dock.

"In addition, we found Gus's fingerprints in Larry McDuff's garage. Remember how we'd requested everyone at the garden party to let us take fingerprints. Well, Gus was one of those who complied.

"Ashley, I called your cell phone repeatedly, trying to warn you to stay away from Moon Gate and Gus."

"Oh, Jon, Ashley," Tiffany wailed, "I'm so sorry for what happened. You could have been killed."

"It wasn't your fault," Jon said, moving closer to her on the sofa and wrapping an arm around her shoulder.

Aha, I thought, so that's the lay of the land these days. Jon and Tiffany. Well, why not? They were both terrific people; both deserved to be happy.

"I know that but I feel responsible," Tiffany said, brushing away tears with her fingertips. "He was my family. If it weren't for me you'd never have met him. I'm the one who got you involved with Moon Gate. But I swear, I didn't suspect a thing."

"Of course you didn't," Jon said soothingly. "Nobody blames you, Tiffany." He reached for a box of tissues and put it in her lap.

Tiffany blew her nose and blotted her cheeks. "I know you don't, but I blame myself. I always knew that Gus was different—so intense, so obsessed with the past, with dwelling on past wrongs. He couldn't let go of old grievances. Yet, I refused to see just how troubled he'd become. He's the only relative I had and I wanted a brother so badly."

I could understand her feelings. I knew how I felt about Melanie.

"So," Tiffany continued, "I turned a blind eye to the scary aspects of his personality. I was into denial. Besides, he'd always been sweet to me, ever since I was little girl. And he adored my mother. She was wonderful to him, and replaced his own. Now he's gone too. It's so hard to believe that he killed Mindy and set it up so that the blame would fall on me."

"He was obsessed, as you say, Tiffany," Nick affirmed.

"You said his fingerprints were in Larry's garage," I reminded Nick. "Are you saying Gus killed Larry too?"

"We believe Gus killed him and tried to make it look like a suicide. It looks like Larry had been blackmailing Mindy. We seized her computer. Her financial records were on it and we discovered that she'd been withdrawing $20,000 in cash each month. What could she possibly have done with that much cash except give it to a blackmailer? Then yesterday, Elaine McDuff came in to see Diane and brought us a bag of cash. Plus someone mailed a compact disk to Diane from a phony address."

I drew in my breath and held it.

"There were photos of Mindy nude on the disk, and we think that somehow McDuff got hold of it, or that he was the person who took the photos—something. Probably, he was blackmailing Mindy over them. Pictures like that would damage her television career and her father's chances of becoming mayor. And on the CD there was a blurry photo of a man."

"Who do you think sent the CD?" I asked.

Nick replied, "My guess is the disk was found by Elaine McDuff. She wasn't sure what it meant, but knowing Mindy was murdered, she felt she had to reveal it, so she mailed it to Diane. Although Elaine denies any knowledge of a disk or of photographs."

I let my breath out.

"So assuming that McDuff was a blackmailer, it wasn't much of a stretch to assume he had tried to blackmail Gus too. There wouldn't be any more money from Mindy, remember; that well had dried up. Elaine swears she never made the tea for Mindy. She said that you, Tiffany, asked her to . . ."

"Oh, yes, I did," Tiffany said.

". . . but that she got distracted by all there was to do and forgot. By the way, how did you know which glass of tea to take to Mindy?"

Tiffany looked thoughtful. "Gus pointed it out to me. It was near him, set apart from the food, on its own little silver tray. He was standing at that end of the table, and he said Elaine had put it there for me."

Nick nodded. "Gus put it there, then stood nearby to make sure no one else inadvertently picked it up. I suspect Larry McDuff saw him set the glass on the table, maybe even saw him bring it from the house. Probably Gus handled it with a napkin or a tissue—his prints were not on the glass—and that made McDuff suspicious."

"Then when it was announced that Mindy had been poisoned," I interrupted, "Larry put two and two together and they added up to $20,000 a month."

"But Gus wasn't going to let anyone blackmail him," Jon said.

"No, he wouldn't have," Tiffany agreed. "He was much too headstrong."

She started to cry again. "If I hadn't seen him do it with my own eyes, I'd never believe he was capable of running into a burning house."

I reached out to her and patted her arm.

"No one thought he'd do such a thing," Nick said. "Certainly not the fireman he was talking to. That man is experiencing a lot of guilt too.

"I have a question for you, Tiffany," Nick continued.

She swallowed hard and said, "What is it?"

"Heather Thorp and Brook Cole swore they overheard you threatening to kill Mindy. Was that true? Because if it wasn't, I'm going to see that those two are prosecuted."

Tiffany hung her head. "I did say it but I didn't mean it. It's just something you say, like, 'Oh, I'd like to wring your neck.' But saying it and doing it are too different things. Mindy was always so ugly to me. At first I tried hard to be her friend, but she wouldn't have it. She thought she was too good for me because of my African-American blood, and she's from one of Wilmington's founding families."

"That's not true," I said. "That's something the Chestertons have told people for so long they probably believe it themselves. The first Nehemiah Chesterton was a carpetbagger, according to Binkie, and he ought to know. He was a greedy opportunist who took advantage of the South's defeat and the loss of so many of our men-folk to grab a shipyard right out of a poor widow's hands.

"According to Binkie, the first Nehemiah Chesterton was in direct competition with your ancestor Caesar Talliere for steam ship building contracts. Gus told me that the finding of Caesar's schooner and his bones confirmed what he had always believed—that the first Chesterton killed the first Talliere. All that violence led to more violence; the sins of the father visited on the sons, like that."

I gave Nick a level look. "I figured out something while I was floating in the lagoon, when the alligator snapped at my foot. It was the alligator that mutilated those corpses that washed up at Fort Fisher. Gus was responsible for their deaths.

"Nem and Janet have been trying to locate their sons. The brothers were supposed to have left with their cousin for a drive to Boulder. I don't think they ever left Wilmington. I think if you compare the DNA of Nem and Janet to the tissue samples you have from those corpses, you will find they are Hugh and Nem the Fourth, and their cousin."

Tiffany let out a long wail and fell back. Hearing just how evil her half-brother had been was too much for her.

Jon gathered her in his arms. "I'm taking you upstairs and putting you to bed."

He looked at me over her head. "Have you got something to help her sleep?"

"There are sleeping pills in the bathroom," I said.

We said goodnight and watched them mount the stairs. If I knew Jon, he'd sit up with her for most of the night.

Nick and I returned to the library and cuddled on the sofa. I borrowed his warmth and his strength.

"I'm sorry, baby, my world can get so ugly."

"It's my world too, Nick, don't shut me out. We've got to rise above this, to take our happiness where we find it."

"You're right. And I think it's time for you and me to claim our happiness together."

I kissed him on the cheek. "I'm all for that. But, Nick, we have to decide where we're going to live, who will be the one to move."

"I know how you feel about Wilmington, Ashley, how you love your home. I could be very happy living here in this house with you. The truth is I didn't much care for Atlanta—too big. And I missed my buddies on the force. Well, it seems I was missed too. They want me back. They've offered me the job of liaison between Wilmington PD and Homeland Security. It'll mean some overnight trips to D.C., but other than that, this will be home base.

"So, Ashley darling, this is a proposal. Will you marry me?"

32

On the first Saturday in May our wedding party assembled on Wrightsville Beach. The wedding and the reception, and an ocean-view cottage for a two-week honeymoon were Melanie's gifts to us. With multi-level decks and a long boardwalk that skimmed the dunes, the house wasn't exactly what I'd call a cottage, but that's the way they do things in the high-end real estate business. The "beach cottage" had four bedrooms, four bathrooms, a high-tech kitchen where Elaine McDuff and her crew were preparing the reception dinner, and a spacious greatroom with a wood-burning fireplace for cool nights.

"This place is heavenly," I told Melanie as she made last-minute adjustments to my gown. I'd lost enough weight so that I fit into Mama's wedding gown, and it was beautiful with a train that would trail behind me over the white runner that had been rolled across the strand.

We hugged and kissed and I thanked her again for making all the wedding preparations. "I was thrilled to do it," she said. "You know I'm good at organizing events, although I've never planned a wedding before."

"I'm wondering when you'll be planning yours," I said, as she arranged the veil over my face.

"Oh, shug, who knows? Don't worry about it. I'm happy with my life the way it is." She grinned wickedly. "I like playing the field. The grass is always greener, and all that. Marriage would cramp my style."

"That's just what I'm worried about, Mel, will it cramp *my* style? I've lived alone for a couple of years now. I'm used to doing things my own way."

"I just want you to be happy, baby sister. Nick's a great guy and he loves you. Why, he wrestled an alligator for you, for pity sakes."

My nervous laughter erupted like a hoot. "Tell me something, sister mine, are you sleeping with Mickey Ballantine? Nick says he's bad news."

Melanie acted outraged. "Who, me? Sleep with two men at the same time?"

I stared at her.

She giggled. "No, I'm not sleeping with Mickey Ballantine. But . . ." and she held up a finger, "I can't promise you I never will."

"Oh, Melanie."

She grinned. "Oh, Ashley."

"By the way, Nem Chesterton withdrew from the race. Did you hear that?" I asked her.

"I did. He's lost his children, the poor man. I suspect he's ruined. Now I want you to forget all about that stuff. This is your day, yours and Nick's and I've worked too hard for you to spoil it with thoughts of homicide and family feuds. Now, come on," she said, "let's go downstairs before Binkie wears a path in the greatroom carpet."

I must have floated down the stairs because I couldn't feel the treads under my feet. Binkie, who was giving me away, paced the floor like he might indeed wear out the carpeting.

He gasped when he saw me, and tears shone in his eyes. "Oh! Ashley dear, you're beautiful."

"It's Mama's dress," I said shyly. I wasn't used to being the center of attention. "I'm nervous," I confided.

Behind me, Melanie said, "She'll be fine."

Binkie said, "I happen to know that Nick is a nervous wreck, and Jon, his best man, isn't much better." He offered me his arm. "Shall we go out now, Ashley dear, and settle their nerves?"

"Yes," I replied.

Melanie led our procession across the boardwalk and over the dunes, looking elegant in a pale blue gown. Watching her step daintily onto the white runner, my heart overflowed with love for my older sister who, when the chips were down, was always there for me.

Guests turned in their folding chairs to watch Melanie march slowly and rhythmically toward the ocean as a recording of Pachelbel's *Canon* played.

A white canopy had been erected midway down the beach, and the tails of gigantic white bows fluttered in the ocean breeze as playfully as the tails of a child's kite. Huge white baskets held mounds of white hydrangeas, and they were banked at the edges of the white carpet that covered the sand under the canopy.

The sun was setting, casting red and gold rays over the scene and tinting white foam to pink. In the east, the horizon had deepened from bright blue to indigo.

When the music switched from Pachelbel to *Lohengrin*, people rose up out of their chairs, oohing and aahing. Binkie said in my ear, "Ready?"

I whispered yes and we started down the aisle that was formed by Nick's friends and mine. Out of the corner of my eye, I saw Tiffany. She'd lost everything, her family home, her brother. All she had left of the Talliere legacy was Caesar's journal, and she was giving that to Beverly Tetterton for the North Carolina Room at the library. And now that she had the leading role on *Dolphin's Cove*, she was making plans to build a house on the Talliere land. The gardens had not been harmed.

I saw Cameron, friends from the historical society, and preservation friends. Everyone was beaming at me, and I could see from their hopeful expressions that they were wishing me happiness.

Then I caught sight of Nick, waiting expectantly under the canopy, and the corners of my mouth turned up in a great big goofy smile.

We reached the first row and there was Mama, so sweet in her pink dress, crying softly. I knew she was missing Daddy, for I was missing him terribly. Aunt Ruby, at Mama's side, blew me a kiss, and before I knew it I was swept along to Nick's side and we were standing together, facing the minister.

Father Andrew intoned the familiar, "Dearly beloved . . . " but the words flowed over me, swallowed up by the resounding surge of the ocean, ebbing gently at the shore.

If Daddy is watching me from heaven, I thought, I know he's giving me his blessing. I know he is happy that I've found a good man to love, someone who will cherish me and protect me as he always did.

I felt Binkie step back to take a seat next to Aunt Ruby, the woman he had loved since childhood.

And then Jon was handing Nick the rings, and he too moved out of my range of vision. There was only Nick and I, Father Andrew, and beyond him, the vast and everlasting Atlantic.

Nick turned to face me, to look deeply into my eyes, as he repeated his vows, faithfully promising to love, honor, and cherish me for all the days of our lives.

Then it was my turn, and as my gaze rested on Nick's wonderful face, his loving hazel eyes, I repeated after Father Andrew:

"I, Ashley Wilkes, take you Nicholas Yost to be my wedded husband. And I do promise and covenant, before God and these witnesses..."

I felt a great rush of joy deep in my soul.

". . . to be your loving and faithful wife, in plenty and in want, in joy and in sorrow, in sickness and in health, and I do promise to refrain from meddling in your homicide cases, for as long as we both shall live."

I heard light laughter, then realized with a start what I'd just promised to do. I laughed too, but I was thinking, *Nick, you little devil, you got the minister to insert those words.*

Nick's gorgeous eyes twinkled and he dimpled, and I melted. Silently, I prayed I'd always melt when he looked at me that way.

I turned to the minister and asked, "May I kiss the groom."

"You may," he said, grinning with amusement.

So I did.

ORDER FORM

Your name: ______________________________

Your shipping address: ______________________________

City: ______________________ State: ________ ZIP: __________

Email address: ______________________________

Please indicate your choices:

___MURDER ON THE CANDLELIGHT TOUR ($12.99)
___MURDER AT THE AZALEA FESTIVAL ($15.00)
___MURDER ON THE GHOST WALK ($15.00)

Take any two books for $25.00, a set of three for $35.00.

Add shipping: 1 book = $2.50
2 books = $4.50
3 books = $6.00

Total: $__________

Make check payable and send to:
Ellen Hunter
P.O. Box 38041
Greensboro, NC 27438

Or order through Pay Pal on my web site:
www.ellenhunter.com

Please allow 30 days for receipt.
THANK YOU!